MR. DOYLE & DR. BELL

Howard Engel

A Victorian Mystery

VIKING

VIKING
Published by the Penguin Group
Penguin Books Canada Ltd, 10 Alcorn Avenue, Toronto,
Ontario, Canada M4V 3B2
Penguin Books Ltd, 27 Wrights Lane, London W8 5TZ, England
Viking Penguin, a division of Penguin Books USA Inc., 375 Hudson
Street, New York, New York 10014, U.S.A.
Penguin Books Australia Ltd, Ringwood, Victoria, Australia
Penguin Books (NZ) Ltd, cnr Rosedale and Airborne Roads, Albany,
Auckland 1310, New Zealand

Penguin Books Ltd, Registered Offices: Harmondsworth,
Middlesex, England

First published 1997

1 3 5 7 9 10 8 6 4 2
Copyright © Howard Engel, 1997

Printed and bound in Canada on acid free paper ∞

Canadian Cataloguing in Publication Data

Engel, Howard, 1931–
Mr. Doyle & Dr. Bell

ISBN 0-670-87755-7

1. Doyle, Arthur Conan, Sir, 1859–1930—Fiction. 2. Bell, Joseph,
1837–1911—Fiction. I. Title. II. Title: Mr. Doyle and Dr. Bell.

PS8559.N49M57 1997   C813'.54   C97-930567-5
PR9199.3.E53M57 1997

Visit Penguin Canada's web site at **www.penguin.ca**

*This book is dedicated to the memory of
Julian Symons*

MR. DOYLE & DR. BELL

1879
Autumn

ONE

In the year 1879, I had not yet completed my medical studies at Edinburgh University. My time was occupied in staving off the tedium of botany, chemistry, anatomy, physiology and the rest of the attendant evils of the healing arts. I achieved this by burying myself in mastering them. It was a life punctuated by the striking of the twelve-o'clock bell from Tran church, the climbing of stairs to watch Sir William Turner remove a metacarpus or resect a carbuncle or two, and refreshed by the occasional glass of sherry at Rutherford's bar in Drummond Street to relive with a fellow sufferer the moments of a deathless lecture on the morphology and properties of the islets of Langerhans. To say that I was going sour on the prospect of becoming a country doctor is to understate the case. It had never been my idea in the first place. It was a matter of necessary expediency, in the light of my father's increasing inability to support his large family.

We came from aristocratic Norman French traditions. The name was originally spelled D'oyly, D'oel, D'Oil and other variations on the same theme. It finally settled on Doyle and Doyle it has remained. Both in France and later in Ireland, where a branch of the family put down roots, we were esteemed an ardent Catholic family. Most Irishmen take us for Leinster Doyles, but we are unrelated either to the M'Dowells of Ireland, of which Doyle is a variant, or the M'Dougalls of Scotland. When we had been forbidden the land under the harsh religious laws in practice then against Roman Catholics in Ireland, to everyone's surprise,

we burgeoned out in the arts. My grandfather was a celebrated portrait painter and caricaturist, my uncles all were
artists and illustrators. One designed the cover of *Punch*,
another was director of the National Gallery of Ireland in
Dublin. Only my father was a practical man of affairs, a
clerk in the Edinburgh Board of Works.

These changes in the family fortunes put a scowl on the
crowned stag in the family crest, but we were apparently
supported by the motto *Fortitudine vincit*. While medicine
was respected around the family hearth, it was not a traditional profession among us.

In spite of this I continued to struggle with Materia
Medica and Therapeutics, only grousing about it at
Rutherford's to Stevenson, who was a good listener with a
dram in his hand. Stevenson was my senior by nearly ten
years, but we had fallen in together when he was having
difficulties similar to my own, first with engineering, where
he was expected to perform up to the traditional standards
of his forebears, who had made the designing and construction of lighthouses a family mystery, and then with the
law, which he liked no better. He had had his initial call to
the bar, but proclaimed that Rutherford's was to be his
chosen bar from then on. Our taste in books was miles
apart, but we were both inveterate devourers of literature
of all kinds and fought about our favourites by the hour.
Our own small literary successes were known to one another,
but seldom mentioned. To be frank, Louis was restless in
Edinburgh and had plans to sail off to America in pursuit
of someone named Fanny. He was just returned from
France, so there was much to discuss.

"Why don't you chuck it all, Doyle, old chap? Cut
loose, raise your sail and be off!" We were seated at a
corner of the saloon bar, facing one another above the
mahogany counter: I with a satchel of notebooks at my feet

and Stevenson with his long legs bunched up, making tenuous his purchase on the stool he was perched upon. Dressed in his accustomed bohemian *déshabillé*, a black shirt with a knotted artist's tie under a velvet jacket, he looked sallow and gaunt. He resembled nothing so much as a corpse animated by the desire to complete what he had set out to accomplish before surrendering himself to the sexton at Greyfriars. His appearance was not improved by strong drink, of which he had already liberally partaken.

With his usual happy perspicuity, Louis had read my mood. I had been taken to task roundly for an assignment which had not pleased my teacher. The event had coloured the rest of the afternoon and was now casting a shadow on the evening as well. Caught out in this way, and attempting to mislead my friend, I tried to imagine that there was a bright side to my situation.

"I'm beginning to see, Stevenson, that I'm not without advantages. If directed properly, they could lead to great success," I said.

"Hacking off limbs, prescribing 'the mixture,' 'the gargle,' 'the tablets,' 'the expectorant'?" Stevenson set down his glass hard on the counter, misjudging its location by two inches.

"It's all very well for you to pooh-pooh my plight, Stevenson: you've a rich father who dotes on you. I'm wearing darned socks that make Lord Nelson's pair at Greenwich look brand new. If I don't play the juggins, if I don't ship out on an Arctic whaler looking for Franklin's bones, if I put in ten years of solid work smelling faeces and measuring urine, I might with luck step into an honorary surgeonship, stifling my dreams of writing stories with an occasional piece sent to *The Lancet*. Now, I ask you, my dear chap, is that the stuff that dreams are made on?"

"Put like that, old fellow, you have won a drop of

sympathy. But, I suspect that it has nothing whatever to do with medicine. You've been imbibing the surrounding Calvinism, that's all. This city is built on the bones of Covenanters. It creeps into our souls while we sleep. We're always looking at the dark side of the moon. As a proper Papist, you should know that. Didn't the Jesuits teach you anything?"

"It has nothing to do with religion, or even with the gloom of this place." Louis and I had long ago spoken of our religious doubts. It only remained to discover which of us was the most absolute agnostic. We had each of us shocked our doting families with unnecessary declarations of our loss of faith. When I think now of the pain we caused our parents, I weep. The unalloyed honesty to which youth is addicted when it finally abandons the hopeless practice of telling lies is no great improvement.

For a moment my friend was distracted as he watched the bar wench refill his glass. She was an attractive lass and not unknown to my friend, who impeded her progress with one familiarity after another. It was with astonishing grace that she moved her slender form from his embrace. Before leaving, and in the same balletic movement, she planted a tender kiss on Stevenson's forehead. Stevenson murmured the name Kate as he caught her to him again. Over his shoulder she gave me a smile that was both wise and weary.

When he'd taken a sip, he turned to examine me again. I cannot imagine what he saw besides my rather outsize form, a purple mouse under my right eye—the result of a recent bout of boxing—my experimental moustache and the glow of much needed conviviality.

"Is there no hope for this patient?" Stevenson demanded, perhaps more loudly than he had intended. "Is he condemned to the birthing stool and the leech jar forever? Are suppuration and decay to be his reward?"

"That's up to Joe Bell."

"Ah! How old Joe?"

"Forty-one or -two, I should think."

"I meant to say how *is* old Joe?"

"Oh, he'll do. With Professor Fraser, he's the most interesting of all my teachers. He picks up your hand and tells you that you just arrived on a clipper from Van Diemen's Land, then explains that only there do such blisters exist. You know he asked me to run his out-patients' clinic for him. You were away in France when that was settled. I've been doing it since last spring."

"A singular mark of distinction, sir. My congratulations, Dr Doyle!"

"Yes, I was surprised he wanted me. It is a bit like going with him on general rounds, only better."

From Rutherford's bar Stevenson and I found a bite of supper in a crowded cellar near the Castle and, after another bottle of wine, he insisted he wanted to walk to Arthur's Seat to look out over the city. He wanted to show me the New Gaol. From there during daylight, you could catch a glimpse of the female prisoners at exercise, looking, he said, like strings of nuns at play. I put him off with a stroll through the streets, shiny with rain. On the way past St Giles's, which was shrouded by hoardings while restoration work was being prosecuted, he performed a mischief near the supposed grave of John Knox in Parliament Square, explaining it was in penance for anything he might have said at Rutherford's that showed disrespect for my religion. As he refastened his buttons, I explained to him:

"The religion of my fathers, old chap, as I have told you many times before, and which you would remember if your head were less befuddled, isn't what I practise."

"Indeed? Then what do you practise?"

"At the moment, nothing. And it suits me very well. I

have difficulty believing that all the soldiers slaughtered at Waterloo and Balaclava have simply ceased to be, but I have no credo that will explain it. In the meanwhile, I have suspended all belief. I recommend it."

"You've become a Nihilist or perhaps a follower of that German chap, Nietzsche. Fellow in search of the super-man." Stevenson looked at me with his head tilted quizzi-cally. For a moment he concentrated upon correcting an error in buttoning. At last he looked back at the plaque in the wall of the church. "When I think of the gallons of blood spilled in the name of religion where we are stand-ing, I am inclined to agree with you and other pessimists. So, I take back the name Papist I gave you. But, what you told me comes under the heading of a private fact. Here in Auld Reekie facts come in two kinds, public and private. The truths confessed in confidence over a glass of sherry at night will be hotly denied in daylight. It is the conven-tional hypocrisy that allows Edinburgh to function even as badly as it does."

"Now it's my turn to put to you the charge of Calvin-ist pessimism."

"Oh, Dr Doyle. The times are out of joint. Either they are or we are. I leave for America in a week. The times may be out of joint there as well, but there will be the novelty of new times and new joints. And there'll be Fanny!"

When we tired of watching Princes Street, black with traf-fic even at that hour, I helped him home through the tall, dark streets to Heriot Row. Beyond the reach of the street lamps and the occasional glim burning behind closed curtains where some tormented soul perhaps could not find sleep, the inky night held us fast. Louis was rather far gone with drink and kept calling on two females of his acquaintance, the afore-mentioned Fanny and someone named Modestine. He invoked them both to carry him off to a happier land.

TWO

The following morning I was early in calling upon Dr Bell at the Infirmary. He greeted me curtly with a shake of his head. "My dear boy, 'That quaffing and drinking will undo you.'"

"Sir?"

"Don't feign ignorance with me, Mr Doyle. Stand up for yourself. Or study to assume the manner of offended dignity with more assurance. Very useful. You may have noticed that I do not wear the blue ribbon of the total abstainer myself. You must not blunder into Crum Brown's presence though. And Professor Maclagan would turn you out. The stain on your tie smells of sherry. Rutherford's, I expect. And then you went to a cellar for supper. The sawdust on your shoes gives that away. But, I'm not here to teach a moral lesson. Fetch the book and see who is waiting outside."

Dr Joseph Bell was the current Bell at the Edinburgh School of Medicine. There had been generations of them before him, some distinguished enough to have their names printed in the annals of the university. Their painted likenesses stared down at one from staircases and along the dark corridors. Dr Joe brought the requisite amount of distinction with him, but had shunned the professorial devices, such as aloofness and mordant sarcasm, that marred the behaviour of many of his contemporaries at the university. Many professors allowed the pales and forts of frosty aloofness to melt by the time students had penetrated as far as their fourth year under their tutelage. Some of them had even mastered a few of our names by that time. But Joseph Bell knew us all by name in our first year. He did not ape his fellows by ridiculing the giver of a foolish answer. A stupid or thoughtless reply raised a question in Bell that meant, here is a problem to be looked into. To say that he was loved does not overstate the case. But he was loved as an actor upon a stage is loved in a favourite part. We enjoyed his eyes that seemed to see everything. We imitated his approach in arriving at a diagnosis, carefully peeling away the layers of irrelevancy until the heart of the problem stood revealed for all to see.

Physically, Dr Bell was not at all prepossessing. True, he was tall, easily six feet in height, but since he lacked a military carriage, and tended to stoop and loll in his chair, he appeared to be a much shorter man. His head was dolichocephalic, that is to say long rather than broad, with a sharp, hawklike nose that kept asunder two penetrating grey eyes. His mouth showed sensitivity, his clothes, conservative in origin, were made comfortable by neglect. His long bony fingers would seem to have done honour to a virtuoso of the pianoforte or violin until they were seen in the operating theatre with dozens of pairs of eyes staring down at the pure music of his lancet. Few of us, not even newcomers, fainted at his operations, for he explained the art of drawing imaginary sheets across the body, so that only the exposed portion needed to be kept in focus. His technique was almost musical, like a great violinist on an Amati.

After quizzing the men and women in the waiting-room, I brought the book back into the surgery and handed it to him. "Try to remember, Doyle, that we are dealing with people here, not gall bladders and prolapsed uteri. We treat the whole patient, not merely the diseased organs."

I ushered in the first of the patients, a man in a new

suit, wearing a brushed beaver hat tilted at a jaunty angle. I moved him towards a chair in the middle of the consulting-room. By now, of course, the room was full of second-, third- and fourth-year students standing by with their notebooks held as though to catch the last words of some expiring monarch. Dr Bell approached the patient amiably. "Well, my friend, I see that you've done your duty by the Queen. Served in the army, have you?"

"Aye, sir," said the patient, removing his hat and placing it on the floor beside him.

"You haven't been discharged very long."

"No, sir."

"You were in a Highland regiment, I expect?"

"Aye, sir."

"Perhaps a non-commissioned officer?"

"Aye, sir." The man's mouth had slowly been dropping open as though the muscles operating the mandible had been severed.

"How did you get on with the weather where you were stationed in Barbados? It was Barbados, wasn't it?"

"Aye, sir."

Dr Bell turned away from the patient to look around the room. He placed a friendly hand on the man's shoulder. "You see, gentlemen," he said to all of us in the crowded room, "the man was respectful, but he did not remove his hat upon entering. They do not uncover in the army. Had he been out of uniform for a long time, he would have learned our ways. So, his discharge is of recent date. He has the air of authority, and he is obviously a Scot. As to Barbados, I see from the book that his complaint is elephantiasis, which is a complaint of the West Indies." We all looked at one another in awe at the miracle that had just unfolded. With his explanation, he had turned the miraculous into a simple parlour trick which even the dullest of us could master with a few days' practice. But this was a trick in itself. The true artist brings off his most difficult feat in making the impossible appear to be child's play.

After the first patient had been examined and his disease made the excuse for a short lecture on the symptoms, cause and treatment of the cumbersome and painful infirmity, I brought in the next patient. He provided the excuse for a homily on the care of the prostate gland. "In youth it is smooth, gentlemen, but as the body ages, it develops irregularities. Palpating it in the usual way will tell you about seventy per cent of its secrets. The remaining thirty per cent are turned away from your enquiring finger. Happily, when a cancer develops, I have found that in most cases, it presents itself within reach of your digits."

As the morning advanced, I ushered in the rest of the patients, one after another, until the waiting-room was quite empty. In almost every case, Bell's eyes had seen what ours had missed. The rounded soles of boots, the stick-pins in neckties, the stains on fingernails, the shine of wear on a pair of trousers, all told tales for those of us who could read them, he taught us. And most of us remembered these demonstrations of the amazing Dr Bell at least until we took our degrees in medicine. Some of us will never forget.

When the waiting-room had been emptied and the surgery put back in order, Dr Bell poured an ounce of a pale amber distillate from a Florence flask into test-tubes and handed one of them to me. "Have a wee dram before you go, Doyle."

"Thank you, sir." I sniffed at the test-tube and noted alcohol and peat.

"Your health, laddie," he said, sipping at his drink. "A cousin makes this on the slopes in the shade of the Sow of Athole. Smell the heather in it." I hadn't expected to be treated to a drink of spirits by my professor and I was flattered by his attention. He looked at me over the top of his drink and began dissecting me, or so I thought.

"You're a stuffy, unbending sort for an Irishman, Doyle."

"I'm an Edinburgh native," I reminded him.

"Oh, I know that," he said, waving his hands as though to muddle what was already clear. "I *know* that. But Scotland has left very little of the Irish of your ancestors about your bones. You've got oatmeal in your blood like the rest of us. Where are your dark Celtic longings, your impossible quests for Cúchulainn and Queen Medb?"

"Sir, I—"

"Ach, call me Joe, laddie. That's my name when I'm not on a platform. I suspect you do already behind my back. I detect in you fine makings, Doyle. But I'm not certain that these are the makings of a country doctor. Or even a fashionable city physician. You've a curious mind. Not the most curious I've encountered, but you're wide awake and bright. You know that the heart is a muscle, but you've heard enough philosophy to wonder what else it is. You know that the sacrum is a composite of ankylosed vertebrae forming the back of the pelvis, but you know that it is so called because it is thought to be the repository of the soul. Have you encountered the soul in your anatomy classes, laddie?"

"No, sir."

"Ha! Nor will you. Will a brass plate outside your door under a red lamp satisfy what you want out of this life, Mr Doyle?"

"I—"

"I say 'this life' out of habit. We look at the world through conventional lenses, laddie. I canna, myself, see you as a general practitioner of medicine. Will you be content to sit in your consulting-room, waiting for your patients to arrive? For listen, my friend, a waiting-room in a fine house in a fine London Street, Cavendish Square, I should guess you're thinking of, is not where patients await the doctor, but where the doctor waits for something to come along. The only thing you can count on is the rent collector, who is never late.

"Perhaps you're thinking of taking up a speciality: eyes, ears, nose and throat; the chest; the brain. All well and good and room to expand. But what says the little manikin under your ribs? What says the darkness of your room to your ear as it lies on its pillow?"

"I had thought—"

"Yes? Yes?"

"I've always wanted to write."

"To write? About what? Since you claim to enjoy literary interests, you might try reading authors who were physicians: men like Sir Thomas Browne, Montaigne, Locke and Holmes."

"Holmes? I don't think I know a Holmes, sir."

"Holmes, Oliver Wendell, professor of anatomy at Harvard. Excellent stuff. If the sort of writing that interests you has aught to do with medical subjects, I'll consider your work for the *Medical Journal*. I can promise you that. But that's not it, is it? I begin to see the Irish coming out in you. It's more than the common Celtic strain, of which we both partake; it's more. Tell me about it. At last I let you open your mouth to speak."

I explained to Bell, after my fashion, which tends to be rather under the mark, about my ambitions in the direction of literature. I told him of the small items I had penned and the letters about them I had received from editors. All the while, Bell nodded, replenished our test-tubes and began filling his meerschaum pipe with shag.

The story of my life, my hopes and ambitions was droning on, quite to the delight of the speaker and the apparent interest of the sole listener, when a noise was heard in the waiting-room. I had forgotten to fasten the outside door. We both got up and repaired in the direction of the sound. The waiting-room was empty except for the figure upon which both of us clapped our eyes. It was a youth of about my own years. His face was marked by confusion and fear. Blood caked in his hair spoke of some injury, the fact that it still ran down the side of his face suggested that it had happened less than an hour ago. His eyes, which sat deep in their sockets, looked from one of our faces to the other. At last he spoke.

"Dr Bell? Dr Joseph Bell? I am a dead man if you fail to help me."

THREE

It was with some difficulty that we managed to half-drag, half-carry the young man into the surgery, for almost as he spoke the words which filled me with dread and curiosity, he fell into a faint.

"Put him down on the examining-table," Bell said firmly, trying to steady his voice. Together we lowered him to the wooden surface I had just re-covered with brown paper. Carefully Dr Bell examined the young man's head. "Get me something to clean away this blood, and scissors to cut his hair." I found what was needed and brought them as quickly as I could to the doctor, who, without looking away from his patient, began snipping away at the blood-matted hair.

"Does it appear to be serious?" I asked, holding my breath.

"It doesn't seem to be. It may be a concussion. We will see. We will see. A length of cotton gauze, Mr Doyle." I supplied him as before and watched the man's closed eyes as they began to flicker in an attempt to return to consciousness. As Bell stepped back, I could see that the wound appeared to be superficial enough: such as might have been caused by a blow from a club or missile. After applying some carbolic, Bell bandaged the head using sticking plaster over gauze. As he completed the work, I could see that another pair of eyes were watching his hands. The man groaned several times, rubbed his eyes and looked about him. He caught both of us in an uncomfortable gaze before he spoke.

"Have I the pleasure of addressing the illustrious Dr

Joseph Bell?" he asked. Bell smiled at the adjective, but decided to postpone any debate about the degree of his celebrity until we had learned more about our visitor.

"This is my assistant, Dr Arthur Conan Doyle. Perhaps, sir, you would tell us your name and give us some reason for your coming here. It's a long way from Market Square and there are doctors' brass plaques outside several of the doors and at least two casualty infirmaries. A man in your condition should have sought the nearest source of care, but you came here, sir." As he said this, he poured a draught of some solution into a beaker and aided the visitor in holding it to his mouth. The man took a sip or two, then pulled his head back. I was glad to see that Bell had not poured from the same source that we had been tapping earlier.

"Dr Bell, I am not a medical man—"

"Of course you're not. You are a painter. Your shoes tell me that much. But you haven't been painting today. You've been making a visit, something official, people you are frightened of, or at least want to make an impression upon. Now, please go on."

"I know enough to be sure that my condition is not serious. Nor is it the chief reason why I sought you out."

"Indeed! Perhaps you had better explain yourself, young man. But first, let me help you to sit up. It is a nasty bump you've had, but, as you say, it is superficial. It will heal and be itself." Together we helped the man off the table and to the only comfortable chair in the surgery. He settled in, looked at our faces again in turn, and then began to speak.

"My name is Graeme Lambert. My grandfather was John Angus Lambert, DD, Principal of the Royal High School until his death three years ago. My father, a broker on the exchange, rejoices in his father's name and blameless character. I have always been one of the two black sheep of the family. Of my brother, I'll speak in a moment. My family has found it has no capacity to deal with artists or with wastrels. It doesn't know where to put us. Things have been somewhat easier since the death of my grandfather, but I have been a son to my parents at arm's length. Only my sister, Louise, has reserved her judgment and has remained in touch with me. I'm sure she disapproves, but her character is such that she overcomes her misgivings. What I mean to say is that I am an ordinary sort of chap, but quite beyond the pale of society. Apart from my brother and me, we are a conventional family in this chillingly conventional city.

"I have been working with an engraver, who has helped to keep me alive, and one of the papers makes use of my political sketches and caricatures. I am, thus, neither wealthy nor starving. I exist, or rather I used to exist, for my work: portraits, which come few and far between, and frescos, an art I alone still practise in this city.

"The change to my present, somewhat less than successful, existence began when Alan, my younger brother, was arrested for the cruel murder of Mlle Hermione Clery, the celebrated soprano of the Royal Opera." Here Dr Bell and I exchanged glances. For there were few in this city— nay, in this country—who hadn't read or heard something of the affair. Newspaper headlines had proclaimed it THE EDINBURGH HORROR in large bold type. Hermione Clery and her paramour were found with their throats cut in an upper room of the soprano's lodgings in Coates Crescent. The presses, wherever they turned, both here and in the south, carried the news. It was a sensational case to be sure, and one which I understood was about to be tried in the assizes.

"I have just come from seeing my brother in the cells.

His solicitor has instructed me to keep clear of the trial. It is his belief that my way of life, the irregularity of my household, my very presence, will redound to the disadvantage of my poor brother. There was a small crowd outside the gaol, and when I came out a cry went up and all sorts of brickbats were thrown in my direction. The impact of one of them you have just treated, Doctor. It was a lucky missile; the malice it represents was truly aimed at Alan rather than me. The case has excited the people of this town and it will not abate until after the trial is concluded."

"Why have you come to see me?" Dr Bell asked quietly, fixing our visitor with a steady look.

"But, there is no one else!" he said. "The police will not listen to me. I've written to Sir George Currie, the Lord Advocate, and to the Home Office. I've appealed to the editor of the newspaper I work for; he rewarded me by removing me from the list of his political cartoonists."

"What about your father? What steps has he taken?"

"My sister tells me that he has done everything I have and more. He moves in influential circles. He knows the lawyers and judges. He speaks their language. But, they have done nothing for him. Nothing. That is why—"

"Mr Lambert, I am a doctor. I am something of an authority in the realm of medicine. I have written several monographs which have appeared in *The Lancet* and my work in the operating theatre has been commented upon in that journal, but, my dear sir, you are asking me to step away from what I know into a world I can hardly surmise."

"You are too modest, sir. I have heard how you assisted a nephew of William Temple last year. In a very delicate matter."

"Ah, you know about that? It was a case of mistaken identity. A slight service for an old friend."

"And there was the case of a trained cormorant and a

lighthouse."

"Hardly a case, young man. A little political intrigue, perhaps. Again, my assistance to a friend has been exaggerated. I can do nothing for you."

"They will hang my brother, sir. He is innocent."

"So he very well may be, Mr Lambert. What on earth can I do about it? Suppose you came to me and asked me to build you a cottage, or go upon the links with you for a round of golf. My answer would have been, 'You've come to the wrong man.' I have no skill in these matters, sir."

"What about the business of the green lampshade? The matter was talked of in my club—when I was respectable enough to belong to a club—for several weeks." Here Bell took a deep breath and walked slowly to the window. For a time he played with the bauble dangling at the end of the window cord. Our visitor watched him for some moments before he returned to his pursuit.

"Have you ever watched a hanging, Doctor? I tell you it is not a pretty sight."

"Indeed it is not. Nor has it been for many centuries. I take it that your outrage against the institution of capital punishment is of recent vintage. To be frank, sir, I am unable to help you. How can I help a man I cannot altogether trust?"

"Are you calling me a liar? Are you mad? Desperate I may be, but my credibility is untarnished."

"In general, perhaps, but when caught between the moor and the loch you are somewhat dramatic in your approach to the truth."

"Wherein did I mislead you, Doctor?"

"You said that your life was in danger. Your exact words were, 'I am a dead man if you fail to help me.' Highly dramatic, to be sure, but unfactual. It is your brother's life that is in hazard, not your own. Now, young sir, I heed to your problem, but I can find no firm footing near you. Will you pull at the weft of the truth again when it suits you?" Lambert looked at Bell and then at me. Colour had drained from his features. His mouth opened and closed twice before he began to speak.

"I confess to misleading you. It was unforgivable. It was a cheap theatrical gesture. But consider my cause, my injury, my plight. I promise to speak only the truth, without exaggeration from this time forth."

"It is of little consequence now. I am sorry for your trouble, but I cannot recommend myself as a means of escaping from it. The cases you mentioned were not the adventures you imagine them. They were simply acts of friendship, which hardly put me in a position to hang out a shingle announcing a change in my profession."

"You admit that they were acts of friendship?"

"Need I say it again? But you, sir, have no such claim on me."

I thought I saw the faintest glimmer of a smile on the face of Graeme Lambert. Bell saw it as well. Still he continued to badger the man.

"Why did you come here? What brought you to this door? Don't tell me it was the red lamp outside, or I will be forced to call you a liar again, sir. Any doctor could have mended your broken head. There is something that you have not said. Out with it."

"Sir, I hesitate to say, before a third person, what I would otherwise only reluctantly impart to you."

"Speak, man! Speak your piece! Dr Doyle and I are colleagues. I trust him with my own secrets, why not with yours?" This was the second time Bell had referred to me as "Doctor," a form of address to which I was in no way entitled: a set of formidable examinations lay between me and that appellation. But, let me impede the story no longer. We both watched the face of our visitor.

"Very well. In the autumn of 1854, Dr Bell, you lay in a crowded ward of the fever hospital, suffering from a malady that had not yet been diagnosed."

"Quite right. This is becoming more interesting."

"The doctor assigned to you was my uncle, the late Isa Merriman, MD. During the course of one night, your fever began to rise to a crisis. My uncle, according to his widow, worked over you through the night. In the end, you survived to leave the hospital. Within a fortnight, my uncle was buried in the Greyfriars cemetery."

"Sir, I am confused: are you telling me that your uncle saved my life and that in so doing he sacrificed his own? I have no independent knowledge of either event. I admit that I was despaired of by my family and sent to the fever hospital as a last resort, but of the great sacrifice you name, I can say nothing. How can such things be proven?"

"Sir," I interrupted for the first time, "Dr Bell owes you no favour. What your uncle did, he did with his own free will. No doctor would have done less. You cannot now hold Dr Bell to account, however painful the story be and however needful your present situation. You can demand nothing beyond what we have already done for you. You have our sympathy and good wishes to be sure."

"Your uncle? He had a port-wine stain on his face? Just here?" Bell indicated the right side of his face with the palm of his hand. The stranger nodded. "Then I do remember something of that confused and painful night. I remember him chilling my body with snow that he had brought in from the street. I remember his voice raised, exhorting me to work with him, to try to hold together the reins of sanity. I remember his strong grip on my hands as he washed me down and wiped the sweat from my face. Yes, I remember the man!" Lambert said nothing for a moment. He got to his feet, holding tightly to the chair as he righted himself.

"I have kept you gentlemen too long," he said in a low voice. "I regret what I have just said, sir. It was unfair and unmanly of me to have mentioned my uncle. Please remember that it was my brother's need that prompted such familiarity." He took two steps towards the door. His face was ghastly white, as he went, holding tightly to the examining-table as he passed it. Imagine the cheek of the man. I tried to mediate my growing anger. How could he use such pressure on Dr Bell? It amounted to nothing less than blackmail. I was still giving inner-voice to these rambling thoughts when Lambert reached the door of the surgery. Bell, too, watched his halting progress. At last, he drew in his breath:

"Mr Lambert," he said, "this history of your uncle has proved more than interesting. I perceive your purpose, of course. It was I who raised the issue of friendship and you have used friendship and the debts of friendship masterfully. If you were a jot more clever, I would have nothing further to do with you." Here Bell paused again, rubbing the end of his chin with a knuckle: "Mr Lambert," he said, "I take it that you are acting as an agent for your brother?" Lambert nodded his head in the affirmative. "You may tell him, young sir, that such service as I can provide is at his disposal."

FOUR

Events moved swiftly after that first encounter with Graeme Lambert. Bell despatched me that very day to the free library to pore over the newspaper accounts of the double murder. In that atmosphere of old leather, polished wood and green lampshades, I read every word that had been written about the case and made notes that put to excellent use the training I had received from Bell and the rest of my teachers.

In bald outline, the case unfolded in this wise. At seven o'clock on the evening of Monday, 21st July, the celebrated soprano Hermione Clery and her lover, Gordon Eward, were savagely murdered as they sat in the first-floor drawing-room of the comfortable flat that had been leased to the singer by the opera company pursuant to the agreement the company had made with her. The address in Coates Crescent was an excellent one, only a short distance from the west end of Princes Street, and forming, with Atholl Crescent and the adjacent parkland, a most agreeable prospect, both prestigious and convenient.

Mlle Clery was of Irish origin, but she had studied in Germany with Liszt and had appeared in London, Paris, Berlin and New York in the works of Mozart, Meyerbeer, Donizetti and Gounod to audiences that applauded to the very echo the brilliance of her coloratura flights. Her high notes were unsurpassed by Jenny Lind herself. Her Donna Anna, her Norma, her Lucia were for a decade the talk of the musical world. The very year of her death, she sang before Queen Victoria at Stolzenfels, where Mlle Lind had earlier had one of her triumphs.

Naturally, upon her sudden removal from the scene, the newspapers both here and abroad followed the case avidly. Reporters from Chicago and New York arrived and were put up at great expense in the best hotels, while they fashioned daily stories despatched by the fastest available methods.

Gordon Eward was the most recent of a string of lovers the singer had taken in the course of her short peripatetic life. She had lived quite openly with the young painter Lafleur-Gérard in Paris, where eyebrows were raised even among the bohemians of Montmartre. Eward was not a well-known writer or painter. The dull truth is that he was a clerk in the Board of Works here in Edinburgh, where he audited the accounts of several departments. The newspapers tried to make a hero of romance out of him and failed. There was too much ink on his fingers even for the American press.

Still, Eward was a handsome young fellow, well-spoken by all accounts, and not without some social standing in Scotland. His great-great-grandfather, a Bible-thumping Covenanter, had perished with his flock in a hunger strike near Aberdeen in 1780. His father was a hydraulic engineer best remembered for keeping the Princes Street Gardens drained. Eward's avocation was music, which he had studied privately with Mazzini until his voice proved to be too frail for the concert stage. Mlle Clery had met him in Menton, where both were vacationing. They arrived in Edinburgh separately at the beginning of the season and maintained their liaison with admirable propriety until their deaths made common knowledge of their intimate association.

The crime occurred shortly after Hélène André, the French maid employed by Mlle Clery, went out to buy a newspaper. She was away slightly more than ten minutes, during which time the two were savagely murdered in the drawing-room.

Mlle Clery possessed an estimated ten thousand pounds' worth of jewels in her flat. She was morbidly afraid of robbers, having lost a fortune in gems once before, during her 1875 stay in Berlin. Along with the normal locks and chains, her front door was equipped with double bolts and two patent locks opened by separate keys. In addition to this door on the first floor, there was a street door, which was also kept locked. The ground-floor flat was occupied by a middle-aged couple named Osborne, who were on cordial terms with their illustrious upstairs neighbour.

That night, the Osbornes heard noises overhead; the falling of a heavy weight that made a cracking noise in the ceiling joists. Curious, and in his carpet slippers, William Osborne walked up the stairs to see what was the matter. He rang the bell, but received no answer. He returned to his own rooms to inform his wife and then went up again. Just then, the maid returned with her newspaper. Osborne explained to her what he had heard, which the maid dismissed as the falling of clothes from the indoor clothesline, an explanation which still left Osborne puzzled. Hélène entered the flat, leaving Osborne at the open door while she explored to see if anything was amiss. She went directly to the kitchen. Before she was out of sight, a man emerged from the bedroom. Hélène saw the man, but from behind.

Osborne thought it was a visitor. Having neglected to wear his spectacles, he saw him none too clearly. The man walked towards the front door as Hélène entered the kitchen. He approached Osborne "quite pleasantly," but, on reaching the landing, he bolted down the stairs and out the front door to the street, slamming the door after him.

By this time, the maid had come out of the kitchen and gone into the bedroom. Not until Osborne asked, "Where is Mlle Clery?" did Hélène enter the drawing-room. Here Hélène encountered a sight that was quite outside her experience. Gordon Eward was lying in a stuffed chair, his head thrown back, and his throat opened up with a gash that had cut through all the soft tissues in front of the cervical vertebrae. All of the major blood vessels in the area had been severed. Blood had pooled below his chair, after the first jets had marked the wall and curtains behind him. Curiously, there was very little blood on the body itself. The female victim, dressed in a green negligée, was stretched out on the floor in the middle of the room, as though she was murdered while making for the door. Her wound was similar to the first victim's, without being quite so extensive. The jugular vein was cut, but the other soft tissues remained intact. Her lifeblood had drained from her white neck and soaked through to the carpet. There was no sign of a weapon, nor were there bootmarks in the gore.

Immediately on finding the bodies, Hélène began to scream. Osborne followed the sound and also took in the horror of what could only have been a most outrageous double murder. On recovering from his shock sufficiently, Osborne ran downstairs and out into the street. Nothing was moving. There was no one in sight. He sent his wife for the doctor who lived a few houses down the crescent. Properly shod, he went out again and returned to the scene of the crime with the first constable he encountered on his way along Shandwick Place.

Dr Mathison examined the bodies to be satisfied that both were in fact dead. Meanwhile, the constable found that a jewel box had been opened and that the floor of the bedroom was strewn with precious gems. With the consent of the policeman, the maid stepped out to inform Mr

Thomas Prentice, Mlle Clery's agent, who lived in nearby Canning Street, what had occurred. It was later alleged that she told Mr Prentice that the visitor who left the flat so hurriedly was known to her.

The police took statements from Osborne and Hélène and issued a description of the wanted man as follows:

> A man between thirty-five and forty years of age, 5 feet 7 or 8 inches in height, thick-set, dark hair, with side whiskers; dressed in a light grey overcoat, and dark cloth cap. Cannot be further described.

The information that Hélène knew the visitor did not appear in her statement or in the published description of the suspect.

The following Wednesday the authorities were able to amplify this description when a fourteen-year-old messenger girl came forward saying that she had seen a man run out of the house in Coates Crescent and along towards Princes Street. In fact, the man bumped into her as he ran off in an easterly direction. She added further details to the description, some of which proved at odds with what was known. There was confusion about the colour, style and material of both hat and coat. This led to the police theory that there were *two* assassins, not one.

After collecting the spilled jewellery from the bedroom floor, Hélène André discovered that a crescent-shaped diamond brooch was missing. It proved to be the only valuable piece that had been taken. If the motive for the crime was robbery, few of the papers commented upon the fact that much blood had been shed for very little return. A sketch of the missing piece was circulated along with a revised description of two suspects wanted for questioning.

On the Friday after the murders, a bicycle dealer named Tobias M'Leod visited the Central Police Station. He told a story that led to the arrest of Alan Lambert for the crime. M'Leod stated that a man he knew as Lambert or Lamport had been trying to dispose of a pawn-ticket for a diamond brooch resembling the one described in the circular. A visit by the police to the pawnshop found the article and confirmed the name of the man who had pledged it. Immediately, a circular with Lambert's name on it was placed on view in public places. His name appeared in the press as: someone the police sought for questioning in connection with the murders. On calling around at the man's rooms in Howe Street, the police discovered that the suspect had decamped. He had sold his furnishings, leased his third-floor flat and fled to Liverpool. In Liverpool it was further learned that the man had booked passage for New York, and had indeed left on a steamer for America not long after the crime was committed.

Lambert, it was learned, was a man of good family fallen upon evil days. He was known to have debts with the shopkeepers on the High Street and to have regularly visited a gambling club in India Street. While the police understood him to be a man of no fixed income and something of a good-for-nothing, he had never been brought to book successfully even for petty crimes or misdemeanours. Drunkenness in a public place was the most severe crime for which he had ever been charged.

The police were sure they had their man. The New York police were contacted by trans-Atlantic cable and the man travelling as Alan Lambert was detained in the cells of the Tombs until Inspector Palmer of the Edinburgh police arrived by the next ship with Mr Osborne, Hélène André and Gladys Smith, the little messenger girl. The three witnesses identified Lambert as "the man." Lambert retained an American lawyer, who believed that his client would never be extradited on the evidence provided. Like many a good man before him, and after him, Lambert did not heed counsel. He voluntarily returned to Scotland under arrest, and now faced trial for the double murder in the High Court of Justiciary in Edinburgh.

FIVE

Under instructions from Dr Bell, I attended the trial on each of its four days. Outside in the High Street, throughout the proceedings, news-vendors had set up makeshift kiosks. Knots of interested citizens quickly exchanged copper coins for the latest news of what was happening on the inside. Placards in large black letters screamed their messages in ghastly hyperbole:

EDINBURGH HORROR
CLERY MURDER SENSATION
TRIAL OF DECADE BEGINS TODAY

The largest courtroom in the old Parliament House was stuffed with sensation-seekers, reporters and the curious. This was the High Court of Justiciary, the highest court north of the border. Every true-blooded Scot recalled, on crossing the threshold, that this building once housed an independent Scottish parliament until the Act of Union rendered it superfluous.

As the jury of fifteen men was empanelled, a thunderstorm outside darkened the chamber and added its own sense of foreboding and dread about the man standing isolated and pale in the dock.

The trial afforded me a chance to see displayed all of the pageantry of the law. With the periwigs and gowns, the white tabs and the bits of ermine, the *mise en scène* was calculated to inspire one with awe, reverence and, yes, fear of the majesty of the legal system. I must confess that it had the expected effect on me. Here matters of life and death were to be debated. Here a man's life was in hazard. Yet when I first saw the Lord Advocate in conversation with the Procurator-Fiscal, fussing with his tabs; Adam Veitch, the silk representing Lambert, being instructed by his junior and muffling a secret yawn; the judge in his scarlet robes with dark crosses raised high upon the bench, I quite forgot myself and almost called out, echoing Lewis Carroll: "You're nothing but a pack of cards!" Happily, I did not.

In the corridor outside, witnesses were sitting, talking to their friends or solicitors, some of them quite at ease, others impressed by the height of the ceiling with its hanging chandeliers and the stripes of sunlight crossing the floor and mounting the wall opposite the tall windows. One man, a tall, heavily built fellow with dark wavy hair and a blue chin, stood by the door like a major-domo. He, I was told, was one of the chief prosecution witnesses, a policeman named Webb. During a recess Webb paced the hall outside the courtroom, as one impatient with the slowness of the law. He had the air of being a shepherd to the remaining witnesses. They consulted him from time to time; he dispensed help with authority. Now and then he whispered in the ears of other officials who hurried self-importantly up and down the corridors, with papers in their hands. Of these, I recognized the broad, sweaty face of Keir M'Sween, the deputy chief constable. M'Sween was famous for regularly cleaning out squatters from the narrow, twisting back lanes, wynds and closes of the Old Town.

When I first saw the accused, my immediate thought was: "They have the wrong fellow!" For Lambert in no way resembled the circulated description of either of the wanted men. In my foolishness, I supposed that the trial would quickly exonerate him, since he stood at least six feet in height, was as lean as a post rather than heavy-set, was clean-shaven and rejoiced in abundant dazzling red hair. In no particular did he resemble the descriptions made public by the police or rehearsed time after time in the newspapers. In spite of this, he was the only prisoner in the dock. While the courtroom held its breath, young Lambert stood and in a clear, brittle voice answered the charges levelled at him: "Not guilty!" he said.

At the end of each of my days in court, I repaired to the surgery of Dr Bell and gave him an account of what I had seen and heard. "Be my eyes and ears, Doyle," he had said. "Omit nothing, any more than the eye censors the scene in front of it. Colour what you say, if you must, with your impressions. These are often the findings of the combined senses and must not be ignored. I'm sure you are an excellent observer." Thus he had instructed me, and I went forth with my notebook and pencils each day. After the first long day, I found Dr Bell waiting for me in his office adjoining the surgery. He got up excitedly as I came in and indicated a chair. As he returned to his own, he rubbed his long hands together, interlacing his virtuoso fingers into a comfortable knot. When I had settled myself, he leaned his head over the back in his chair and shut his eyes.

"Tell me about the judge, Lambert's counsel and the Crown prosecutor."

"The judge is a sleepy drone, but not to be disregarded. Lord Cameron is a judge of the lists. I have not seen enough of him to say aught against the man."

"He will defend the values of property and our rather narrow Scots morality, I am sure. Go on."

"The Lord Advocate is a—"

"The Lord Advocate? The Lord Advocate is conducting the case for the Crown? Very interesting! Paint me a picture of him."

"He's a speech-maker, something of a spellbinder. His challenge to a juror sounded like Sir Henry Irving doing Mark Antony; a call for a brief recess was Henry V before Harfleur."

"Excellent! Such a one will trample on the facts to make a rhetorical effect. What's his name?"

"Sir George Currie, QC, LLD."

"Ah! I know the man! From Glasgow. He may be somewhat enamoured of his eloquence, but he's no fool; he's not a bullfrog: full of hot air with no substance. We must watch him. I remember him from years ago. He was ambitious then. He married an iron-merchant's daughter in a ship-building town. Aye, he's a canny one. Wanted to be a law lord before he was fifty. He did it too, not at all impeded by his peptic ulcer. Lambert's counsel had better keep his ears open. What do we know about him?"

"Mr Adam James Veitch, BL, LLB, is an able man—"

"You say that like a fishmonger discovered in the act of giving fair weights. Come to judgment!"

"He's a small terrier barking at the gate, while the thieves come around him laughing into the house. He is well learned in the law, shows up well in cross-examination, but he lacks the experience as well as the authority and eloquence of Currie. This morning, he suppressed a yawn. He may be bored by the case already or he could have been up all night going over the brief."

"Well said. He won't have the starch to interrupt the great man even if he says that the murderer was found concealing a broadsword up one sleeve and a phial of strychnine up the other."

"What's to be done?" I asked.

"Go back to the courtroom tomorrow."

"But, the clinic? Your patients?"

"Doyle, I can dragoon young Biggar to do your work, while you do mine at the Parliament House."

"Oh, there's one thing I forgot. The Procurator-Fiscal was there."

"Ah! Sir William Burnham. His purple face was in full bloom, I suppose?"

"Not at that hour. Perhaps pink from a hot bath."

"Such ostentation!"

"What exactly is a procurator-fiscal? I know vaguely—"

"And 'vaguely' isn't good enough. Right. The Procurator-Fiscal is a public prosecutor. There's one for every shire. He acts as a chief coroner, taking the initiative in cases of sudden or suspicious death. It's a powerful office and Sir William is not a man to be trifled with."

I attended the second as well as the remaining two days of the trial. All of the characters I had discussed with Bell stood out from the others, as though in relief. Inspector Webb and his superior, Deputy Chief M'Sween, were always about in the corridor outside the courtroom or standing up in the back row. Once, I saw Webb with a camera on a tripod outside the Parliament House, making a study of people sheltering from the sudden treat of noonday sun.

In the courtroom, I heard how the accused had been recognized by the three witnesses at the scene and how he had desperately tried to pawn the stolen diamond brooch. He was identified by other witnesses as the man seen loitering in the street on several occasions prior to the crime. It was pointed out that, apart from the highly suspect testimony of a mistress and a servant, the accused could not account for his time for some hours before and after the fatal assault upon Mlle Clery and Gordon Eward. In cross-examining Lambert's servant, the Lord Advocate drew from her the fact that Lambert's mistress sometimes entertained visitors when Lambert was from home. He left the jury with the impression that Lambert was living off the avails of prostitution and otherwise maintaining an existence that was well beyond his means, but also beyond the moral pale of every Scot on the jury.

Sir George did not question witnesses, he assailed them, he flailed them. And as they sputtered in incoherence on the stand, Currie rolled his eyes at the jury, suggesting that the corruption of the witness was so inbred as to render him quite helpless before an honest enquiry into plain facts. "I can, members of the jury, draw seven—yes, seven!—priceless inferences from that last admission. I hope that you will do the same." Or again, he tried to suggest, in his examination of the maid, Hélène André, that the murders were deliberately timed to coincide with her nightly search for the evening paper. To him, this "proved" premeditation. It meant nothing to Sir George that the murderer would have had a better opportunity for his crime if he had committed it on one of the maid's weekly two half-days off. The defence witnesses were savagely bruised by the Lord Advocate. On descending the stand, they fled the courtroom as though being followed by a swarm of revengeful furies.

But in his evidence and cross-examination, the Lord Advocate was merely toying with the witnesses. When it came time for his final address to the jury, he brought out his heavy artillery. He rose to speak after a morning recess and spoke continuously and extemporaneously for two hours. He began in a low voice, resting his left hand on a small pile of books on the table, his right holding a sheaf of paper. "May it please your lordship—gentlemen of the jury, on the evening of the 21st July last, two young people, one a talented and beautiful artist, the other a promising civil

servant, both, as far as we know, without a single enemy in
the world, were found murdered in the upper rooms of the
female victim's dwelling in Coates Crescent of this city. The
two were discovered under circumstances of such savage
ferocity as to beggar all description..."

While he was speaking, no one who heard him was
aware of anything else going on in the world outside. Had
the Parliament House caught fire, we would not have
moved from our seats. He held us like an Irving or a Mes-
mer. We could not choose but hear. He painted a picture of
the accused as a low beast, wallowing in the worst sort of
sin and debauchery, coming from his lair to pluck out the
life of an artist whose talent lay far beyond his stunted
imaginative grasp. He depicted him loitering, planning and
executing the crime. He told how he took the knife he had
brought with him and cut the fairest throat in all the land;
how he had stilled the greatest voice of the century; how he
had blackened the name of this city in all the art capitals of
the world with his deed.

" ... Up to yesterday afternoon," the Lord Advocate
continued, "I should have thought that there was one serious difficulty which confronted you, gentlemen of the
jury—the difficulty of conceiving that there was in existence a human being capable of doing such a dastardly
deed. Gentlemen, that difficulty, I think, was removed
when we heard from the lips of one who seemingly knew
the prisoner better than anyone else, that he had followed
a life which descends to the very lowest depths of human
degradation, for by the universal judgment of mankind, the
man who lives upon the proceeds of prostitution has sunk
to the lowest depths, and all moral sense has been
destroyed and has ceased to exist. That difficulty removed,
I say without hesitation that the man in the dock is capable
of having committed this dastardly outrage..."

His soaring voice went on and on. He reviewed the
evidence, including the brutal, totally unnecessary murder
of Eward, the unexpected second person in the flat when
the maid left to perform an errand. It was magnificent.
When he sat down at last, the instinct to applaud was all
but overpowering. I felt as though I had heard one of the
great actors or preachers of our age. No one spoke for
some time.

Counsel for the accused made a short logical speech
which left no impression at all on the members of the jury.
Even the judge in his summation and charge to the jury carried echoes of the Lord Advocate's mastery. The day concluded with the jury retiring to settle on its verdict.

I recited my account of all this to Bell when he wel-
comed me for the first time into the sitting-room on the
first floor of his house in Lothian Street. It was a rumpled
set of bachelor rooms, with books and papers left on every
available horizontal surface. The walls were lined with
medical books, the table held a microscope and other
scientific apparatus, half-hidden under a discarded dressing-
gown. It was a comfortable, leathern lair showing no hand
of the fair sex in any of its appointments. He offered me a
seat near a window looking out on the museum, where, as
I have said, I related what I had seen and heard without
knowingly gilding the facts.

"And he did all this without a word on paper," I said,
trying, in my enthusiasm, to re-create the feeling in the
courtroom, "without notes of any kind!"

"That," said Bell in a dry whisper, "may account for
the manifold inaccuracies."

"What?"

"In what you have reported to me, I have counted no
fewer than five-and-twenty erroneous statements of fact
and false inferences from the evidence. I am, of course,

relying on the summaries of the evidence you have provided. For instance, in his opening statement, the Lord Advocate said: 'We shall see in the evidence that we shall present
to you how it was that the prisoner came to know that Mlle
Clery was possessed of these jewels.'"

"Yes, I remember that."

"Well, you were in court every day of the trial. Did you
at any time hear him elucidate on that? He promised to
show the jury a connection between the accused and the
singer's jewels. Did he deliver on that promise? Unless you
forgot to tell me, he did not. What is worse, the learned
judge, no Daniel evidently, failed in his summation to
comment on the Lord Advocate's delinquency."

"What is to be done?"

"At the moment? Nothing. If the jury has its wits about
it and uses its eyes as well as its ears, it will find for the
accused. The description of the wanted man bears no
resemblance to the man in the dock. But, as I fear may happen, their ears still ringing with the sound and fury of Sir
George Currie, the Lord Advocate will triumph and our
man will be convicted. Whatever happens, there is nothing
for us to do but wait. In the meantime—"

"Yes, Dr Bell?"

"May I offer you a glass of sherry?"

SIX

The jury considered its verdict for one hour and ten minutes in the morning session, having been closely cloistered overnight. When the jury had entered for the last time, walking to their places with their looks ahead of them and not out into the room, the judge returned to his bench, letting his eyes roam over the courtroom as though he were counting the house. The Clerk of the Court rose. "What is your verdict, gentlemen?"

"The jury, by a majority," said the foreman, glancing at the scrap of paper in his hand, "find the prisoner guilty as libelled."

It found the defendant guilty! The vote was: Guilty, 9; Not Proven, 5; Not Guilty, 1. The courtroom let out the breath it had been holding since the foreman of the jury got to his feet. The man in the dock jumped to his feet. "My lord, may I say a word? Will you allow me to speak?" All voices in the courtroom became mute; all eyes were on the man in the dock.

"Sit down just now," the judge said, when he had found his voice. He nodded to the clerk of the court to continue, to try to rescue the rhythm of the proceedings.

"Then this is your verdict?" the clerk demanded. The foreman nodded his head and then affirmed that it was. With unseemly speed, the junior Crown advocate was on his feet:

"I move for sentence," he said. It was received as though he had shouted an indecency at the bench. A moment later, the prisoner was passionately protesting his innocence, demanding justice and his rights under the law.

"My lord, I came back here on my own account ... I came to defend my right. I know nothing of the affair! You are convicting an innocent man!" The blood fled from the face of the judge. He began to clean his spectacles absently with one of his white tabs.

"I think you ought to advise the prisoner," he said in the direction of Mr Veitch's table, "to reserve anything he has got to say for the Crown authorities." Then, struggling with the two officers who had flanked him, the prisoner was removed from the courtroom down to the cells below. When he had been calmed to a degree, he reappeared in the dock, his knuckles quite white with tension. The judge donned the black cap and solemnly condemned the prisoner at the bar to death by hanging. After the fuss and fury of the trial, the sentence came as a relief to the chief law officers of the Crown, as a shock to many in the courtroom and as a matter of indifference to the judge, to whom it appeared the hearing of capital cases was no different from petty larceny. I tried to find among the expressions on the faces of the jurors which one of the fifteen had not been convinced of poor Lambert's guilt.

I sadly brought this news back to Lothian Street, where Bell accepted it as well as he could.

"Now we must shift our stumps," he said. "Three clear Sundays must pass before the execution," he said. "If tradition is any help, our man will be executed on Thursday, the 23rd."

"Yes," I said. "That was part of the sentence. I should have told you."

"My friend, since there is no regular appeal in Scottish cases, we haven't a moment to lose. We will have to be clever, reading between the lines of the evidence that was presented."

"Between the lines, I don't understand."

"The public record shows what was placed in evidence in the trial. We must assume that some evidence in the possession of the police was not made available to the prosecution and that all of what the prosecution knew was not disclosed to the accused's counsel."

"But that's outrageous!"

"Nevertheless it is common practice in this country. It is well to cultivate a certain cynicism when dealing with the practical side of the law. The theory is all very well. Now, we have no legitimate way of gaining access to such evidence. So, we must tap the sources ourselves."

"Good! Where do we begin?"

"Why, at the pawnshop, my dear fellow. At the pawnshop."

Together we took a cab from the rank in front of the museum to the address I gave the driver, who urged his horse forward without a suspicion that a man's life might hang in the balance of our findings at Aiken's Pawnshop in Rose Street. As we drove, Bell mused to himself, sometimes gnawing at the leather of his glove. "We will never be able to see the precognitions taken by the police! Damnation!"

"Precognitions?"

"The statements the police took down in writing from the witnesses. It was from these that the prosecution built its case. It is a pity that I am not a consulting detective, Doyle. I should otherwise have friends in the police who might have allowed us access to the precognitions. But, our friend Graeme Lambert knew we were neophytes when he took us on. If only the consequences of failure were less severe for his brother. A broken neck is well beyond my healing arts."

The cab rumbled over The Mound, crossing the railway tracks by the National Gallery. From there it was but a short distance to Rose Street, which was noted for its dram shops and public houses. The three tarnished brass balls of Aiken's shop could be seen from afar. Bell paid the cab and we climbed down. A cold wind blew down the street, whipping up fallen leaves lying in the gutters. A bell sounded as I opened the door for my friend.

A middle-aged man wearing thick lenses greeted us with a frown as we approached the caged counter of his establishment. He moved an ormolu clock to the top of a display case.

"Gentlemen, in what way may I serve you?" he said in an oily voice that reminded me of an unsavoury character in Dickens.

"I am sorry to interrupt you at dinner, sir, and, moreover, get you up when you would much prefer to be lying down."

"I beg your pardon? How did you—?"

"Not very difficult, Mr Aiken, if, indeed, you are he. You wear some of your dinner on your waistcoat and chin, and the smell of liniment about you is enough to bowl one over. I can also see that you are favouring your left foot. I will leave you a prescription that might ease the pain, sir."

"But, sir, you did not come here to enquire after my health." It was said as a statement of fact, but intended as a question. Bell smiled at his acuity.

"My friend and I are looking into the particulars of the Lambert case."

"Ah! That poor fellow! I read about the trial in the paper. My neighbour next door has just looked in to say the young man is condemned. He has but three weeks to live and then—" Here, the pawnbroker made a demonstration with his hands and neck of the fate in store for our client on the 23rd. "I knew the young man well, you know. In this business, gentlemen, we meet many different kinds

of people. Who would have thought—?" Again, he left the
thought incomplete except for a pantomime gesture with
his hands.

"Tell me about the brooch he placed in pawn with
you," demanded Bell, with authority enough to concentrate the pawnbroker's ramblings.

"A fine piece," he said. "A very pretty brooch. A work
of art, I assure you."

"When did you first see it?"

"Let me see, let me see." He rubbed his grizzled chin
with the back of his hand, removing traces of his meal incidentally. "I have the date here in my book." He wet his finger with his tongue and began turning over the pages. "Let
me see, let me see," he repeated again and again. At last his
finger stopped in its travels down the columns. "Aye, here
it is."

"Let me see it!" Bell almost barked the command.

The pawnbroker began to turn the ledger around, when
a face came around the corner of the door leading to the
back of the shop.

"What is it, Otto?" demanded a large auburn-haired
woman.

The pawnbroker turned and with evident embarrassment limped across the floor to the woman. For a moment
or two they whispered in a language unknown to me with
evident signs of excitement in both of their voices. The for-
eigner distrusts all invasions. Every knock on the door is a
threat. Together, they regarded Bell and me: representatives
of that alien world that had dogged their nights and days.
"Just one moment, gentlemen, my wife—" Here he indicated unnecessarily the woman frowning at his side. "But
the police have instructed us to be cautious about enquiries
of the kind that you are making. I am sorry, but I don't
think I can assist you further. If I could, believe me I

should—" Again he broke off. No doubt he had noticed that Bell, totally ignoring both of them, had turned the ledger around and was studying it.

"Sir, if you please—"

"Mister, you have no right—" This from the pawn-broker's buxom wife.

Bell paid them no notice whatever. He turned to me: "Doyle, this brooch was placed in pawn three weeks before the murders. It has been here ever since. Tell me," here he looked at the man with the wet, shifty eyes, "tell me at once, what you know about this brooch!"

"I have been cautioned by the police, gentlemen."

"You will be breaking granite in Peterhead with a pick, if you don't tell me what you know!"

"The brooch, he said it was his mother's. It was an heir-loom. I could see he treasured it. I gave him what I could. Not what it is worth, to be sure, but, I am a businessman. I have to use my judgment in these matters. But, you are right, the date is marked on the ticket as well as here in the book."

"Then the police know—have known for more than two months—that this is not the brooch taken from the scene of the crime! The police have had that information in their hands from the very beginning."

"I can't believe it," I muttered.

"If you would please keep our names out of this, gentlemen, it would be appreciated, I assure you."

"The brooch was the only piece of evidence connecting Lambert to the crime. And now we see that that link in the chain has broken. Indeed, it never existed!"

"It was M'Leod, the cycle dealer, who started this," I added, attempting to be helpful. "He said that Lambert was trying to sell the pawn-ticket for ready cash."

"Aye, but the brooch had been in the shop long before

he needed the money the sale of the ticket might have obtained."

"True, sir. He made regular payments on the article until he fled the country," said the pawnbroker. His wife nodded her concurrence.

"Where is the brooch now?" I ventured to ask.

"Oh, sir, the police took it along. 'Evidence' they said."

"A diamond brooch is but a trifle here," said Bell. "Come, Doyle, there's more to be done and none of it here." He turned to the front door, leaving it for me to nod our thanks and leavetaking to the pawnbroker and his wife. I followed Bell into the street as he hailed a cab near the corner of Castle Street. As I climbed up behind him, he sniffed the sharp air. "I begin to scent the fox, Doyle, and we haven't a moment to lose!"

"Where are we going?" I asked, incredulous.

"To Waverley Station to catch the 12:15 train to Liverpool."

SEVEN

In the train, Bell took me over my notes about Lambert's flight from Edinburgh to America. We had the compartment to ourselves for most of the journey, allowing my friend, for so I now deemed my teacher and benefactor, to enjoy his pipe as the train made its way south. Another time I would have marked our progress with greater enjoyment. Apart from occasional glimpses of roofless Gothic arches against the sky, hilltop castles and the estuaries of salmon streams, all of which rescued me from my preoccupations, for the most part the scenery could have been painted on the wall of a cyclorama. I was not in the mood to have my spirits lifted by the works of nature or of man.

Upon arriving at Lime Street, we made our way on foot to the North-Western Hotel, where Lambert had passed his last night of freedom in Britain. The plain Englishness of English faces startled me more here in Liverpool than in London. They were whey-coloured, joyless, drab-eyed, even those that were cleaner than those I encountered daily in the Infirmary waiting-room at home. The walk from the station thoroughly illustrated the comparative meanness of the buildings running down to the busy harbour. In Edinburgh we lived among the ruins of great buildings; here people lived as squalidly, but without the stamp of vanished glory.

Bell procured a double room and we had our supper in a high-ceilinged, spacious restaurant attached to the hotel, where we both fell to with a will after our long journey.

After a meal that satisfied our hunger but left the palate

unelevated, we strolled together down to the docks with their high wooden gates, iron cranes, steel yards and masts for loading goods. We were about to turn around, when we were accosted by a caped policeman who enquired what we were doing wandering near Her Majesty's Docks at that hour. I explained that we were visitors from Scotland taking the air before returning to our hotel.

"And which hotel might that be, sir?" asked the policeman. When I told him, he pulled his cape more securely around him and repeated the name.

"The North-Western! Ha! That's where that young villain from Edinburgh stayed on his escape to America, the one that's for the chop in a few weeks. We'll send old Marwood north to do the job on him. No extra charge."

"Constable, you seem to know a good deal of the affair. I suppose the Edinburgh police sent down a number of officers to look into the matter?" The face of the policeman was as rosy and as shiny as an apple and, with the exception of his moustache, as smooth.

"Aye, they sent their number-one man, Detective-Lieutenant Bryce. I talked to him at the station and report him as fine a man as ever I met."

"I've heard that he is a most conscientious officer," said Dr Bell.

"Queen's Medallist in reward for meritorious services. You may have read about him after the Wilkhaven ferry murder case. It was five, six years ago if I recollect aright."

"It was in 1875," Bell corrected, adding for my sake: "He gave evidence in that trial that disproved the testimony of several so-called 'eye witnesses.' They were out to collect the reward offered by the police. Some of these people will sell their grandams for a mess o'potage."

"As fine an officer as ever you'd care to meet, I say," repeated the constable.

"I dare say, I dare say," mused Bell. "John Ormiston Bryce is all that you say, Constable. That he is makes our work here in Liverpool all the harder."

We took our leave of the policeman, who saluted us smartly. He watched us as we moved away from him and the strong scent of the bay rum he used on his hair. Liverpudlians took their docks seriously. Goodness knows what would have happened to us had he found us in possession of a camera and tripod.

When we arrived back at the hotel, after walking through a light rain, the reception counter was almost deserted. The northern English know their minds, it would seem: those who meant to stop the night had arrived, those who intended to depart were long gone. An assistant manager was at the desk when we approached his suspicious-looking countenance. He busied himself in fastening down the hotel register, whose errant pages were blowing about in the wind which accompanied the sudden shower.

"Mr Arbuthnot," Bell began, reading the name on the empty desk behind the counter, "how are you enjoying your new home in Liverpool? Though you've been here but a short time, I observe that you are getting on well." A shadow came over the man's face as though a fortune-teller in whom he didn't believe had told him of great things to come. He looked about to summon the police.

"Sir?" said he with a hint of incivility. "Am I acquainted with you?"

"You'll find us registered in Room 308. If you are wondering at my knowing your name and former residence, pray allow me to explain: your name is on your desk for all to see. Your suit was made by a tailor in The Lawnmarket in Edinburgh. Nowhere is a lapel cut like that except in Milan, and you, my friend, are no traveller. Arbuthnot is a Scottish name. There are physicians, divines, admirals and famous wits of that name, as you may know. Your tailoring is from Edinburgh, but your linen and necktie are English. From that, I see that you have not been at this work above six months."

"Five and a half, sir. Are you one of the detectives, sir? I was told that I would not be called at the trial, so I wasn't expecting to hear from you again. I see that you got the fellow. A length of rope will give him what he deserves. What a waste he made in cutting off the life of that opera singer, Hermione Clery."

"Aye, a long drop on a short rope will teach him the lesson he deserves. I hope he will profit by it."

"Is it the case that brings you here, sir? I had thought it was over and done with."

"Just checking up on a few things, Mr Arbuthnot. Loose ends, you might say. For instance, do you still have the register where the culprit signed his name?"

"Of course, it's right here." He went to his own desk and produced a ledger identical to the one we had signed upon registering. He quickly thumbed the pages and turned it around for us to see. "There it is, sir. Big as life."

Indeed, there it was:

Alan Lambert, 1 Howe St., Edinburgh
Forward post c/o Cunard Steamships,
New York City, New York, U.S.A.

"Excellent!" said Bell, shutting the book with a loud report. "Tell me, Mr Arbuthnot, didn't Detective-Lieutenant Bryce tell you that the register might be taken and used in evidence?"

"Indeed he did," responded the assistant manager, "but the other policeman—you know, Mr Webb—said that it would not be needed, but to keep it under lock and key all the same. As you see, I am keeping it safe. There's no telling what newspaper reporters and such would do with it. I discussed the matter with Mr Crombie, of the Cunard company, who intimated that he had been given the same warning by Mr Webb. Mr Crombie told me that Detective Bryce was quite put out when he saw that Lambert had signed his own name on the register at their office too. Now, why would that be, sir?"

"It's a question of trying to be cleverer than the police, Mr Arbuthnot. Some villains are that sharp they sign their own names to bad cheques."

"I see, sir."

Bell had raised an eyebrow for me to see when Arbuthnot mentioned Inspector Webb. I remembered his dark presence in the corridor outside the courtroom, as he kept the witnesses together. It was a sombre thought.

A few pleasantries about the weather in Liverpool and the inconvenience of living away from home closed the conversation with the assistant manager of the hotel, who wished us good night after directing us to the saloon bar. Once installed there, I was at last able to speak my mind and unburden the weight of our recent findings. First, we each ordered a local Liverpool ale that the assistant manager had recommended. A few moments after tasting it, I felt calmer and able to put my thoughts into some order.

"Out with it, Doyle. I can see your thoughts are like greyhounds ready to slip their leads. Tell me what you have observed."

"My dear Dr Bell—"

"For God's sake call me by my name when we have the froth of beer on our faces, man! Is it 'Conor' they call you?"

"Conan, if it please you, Joseph."

"As for me, 'Joe' will do the job nicely, Conan. Ah, yes,

your godfather was a Conan, wasn't he? And your family includes the cleverest sketch artist in Britain, the famous Dicky Doyle of *Punch*. Now, let us return to the libretto. You were saying?"

"In just a few hours in Liverpool, we have learned that Alan Lambert, the fleeing assassin, signed his own name to the hotel register, gave his true Edinburgh address and booked a trans-Atlantic ticket in his own name."

"He also aided his pursuers further: he left a trail that led from the hotel to the Cunard booking office. There, tomorrow morning, if Mr Crombie proves as accommodating as Arbuthnot, we will finish in time to catch the afternoon train north."

"But, Joe, this is not the picture of a man escaping from the law!" Bell looked at me curiously, as though I might have answered a question foolishly in the lecture hall.

"Did you expect to find it otherwise?" asked my friend, with a wide grin.

EIGHT

As Bell had guessed, Mr Crombie told us, quite without guile on our parts, that Lambert had purchased the steamer ticket in his own name, had given Howe Street, Edinburgh, as his last address, and asked the company to hold his post until he had established an address in New York. More surprising than this, Crombie said that Lambert's passage had been ordered by post with a deposit of ten pounds three weeks *before* the murders of Mlle Clery and her friend.

In the train on the way back to Edinburgh, Bell was deep in thought. His head thrown back against the seat, he was lost to interruptions less serious than a general derailment. I wanted to review with him the possibilities and implications of the information we had uncovered, but Bell had put himself out of reach. I was, however, able to settle several things for myself without reference to my colleague.

First of all it had become plain that what we had learned, the police could also have learned and had in all probability done so. Yet this information was not presented in evidence at the trial. If the police knew about it, they were obliged to pass that information along to Sir William Burnham, the Procurator-Fiscal, by way of the Chief Constable of Edinburgh. How else would the counsel for the accused find out that the story of the flight from Edinburgh to America was an invention? I made a note to examine upon our return the circumstances of the manner in which our man left Edinburgh. We knew that M'Leod had been approached by Lambert to purchase his pawn-ticket. There was a touch of panic in the picture that conjured up. But there were other things: his chattels, his lease on the Howe Street flat, the closing of bank accounts and so on.

For a moment, I imagined Lambert as some sort of master criminal, such as one reads about in the stories of Poe and Gaboriau. Such a criminal might have provided these clues for us to find. To a man of this sort, nothing is left to chance. Every act is premeditated. With this premise, I reviewed what we knew. Lambert couldn't have known at the time of the murders that his departure from Scotland would be interpreted as flight by the police. Nor could he have guessed that what appeared to be innocent acts would be taken to be anything else. My hypothesis dissolved.

Another matter, also involving the police, was the impression I had been given that there was a dichotomy in the police investigation. Bryce was the first-footer in the case, but Webb came running after him and contradicting what he had said. In fact, Webb, the dark-haired man I had seen with the witnesses at the trial, appears to have bottled up evidence that might have been—nay, would have been!—of use to the defence. Both Arbuthnot and Crombie had been warned by Webb to keep Lambert's openness and can-dour regarding his travelling arrangements as quiet as pos-sible. I noted in my book that I must find out more about both of these law officers and their curiously overlapping investigations. The police will have to be seen through the same microscope as Lambert. If the methods of the police are not to be investigated, the enquiry is futile.

Upon leaving Waverley Station, with the nearly forgot-ten stench of Auld Reekie in my nose again, Bell dropped me within an easy walk of my home, and continued to the university, where he had classes to meet. Bridget, the maid, handed me a note which said that my mother would be from home for the remainder of the day. She was no doubt visiting my father, who had been taken to a nursing hospi-

tal shortly after term began. After bathing and putting on
fresh linen, I returned to the university, where I spent the
rest of the day making excuses for my absence and prepar-
ing slides for a pathology demonstration the following day.
But however engrossing the tissues and sera on my microscope slides, my mind kept wandering back to my non-
medical studies under my remarkable friend.

I thought of the place of the law among us, of what Dr
Johnson had said on his visit to this city about the law and
our courts:

> ... A lawyer is not to tell what he knows to be a
> lie: he is not to produce what he knows to be a
> false deed; but he is not to usurp the province of
> the jury and of the judge, and determine what
> shall be the effect of evidence... A lawyer is to do
> for his client all that his client might fairly do for
> himself, if he could ... If lawyers were to under-
> take no causes till they were sure they were just,
> a man might be precluded altogether from a trial
> of his claim, though, were it judicially examined,
> it might be found a very just claim...

These musings were terminated by the explosion of my
friend Budd into the laboratory. George Budd never
knocked or tiptoed into view, he burst upon the scene like
Macbeth into the company of the witches.

"Doyle, you reprobate! Where have you been? I have
been searching high and low for you!" Here he clapped me
on the back and sat down on the edge of the table, ignoring my slides and notes. George Turnavine Budd was the
son of a distinguished Bristol physician noted for his pio-
neering efforts in the control of typhoid and scarlet fever.
George was noted for nothing whatever except his gigantic

girth, his boundless energy and his sudden enthusiasms. He was like an astronomer who could see no planet but the one he had discovered; a composer whose latest song was the greatest that had ever been written. One night I was awakened by his knock and when admitted he begged me to review with him the texts for an examination we were to sit the next day. He insisted on doing the half of the material I had already gone over rather than the portion I had planned to look at in the morning after a good night's sleep. He never apologized for this invasion, nor did he, to my best recollection, ever refer to it. Budd was a huge man, who had missed getting the Rugby International cap because of his accursed contempt for rules. Let rules rule all the world, George Budd would have none of them. He marched to his own drum and could never understand that many of his problems were of his own making.

"I have been in Liverpool, if it is of any interest."

"Liverpool! Seeking out the vice, old man, when there's so much of it under these very eaves. I tell you I'll swear off drink and adopt the prim countenance of the Primate of Scotland if you can demonstrate where Liverpool excels Auld Reekie in vice. Tell me, man!"

"I was in Liverpool on business," I explained, but recognized with regret that I had once more taken on that cool, limp courtesy that marked all of my dealings with Budd. The plain fact was, I didn't trust him. He was too unpredictable. My reserve in his company came from trying to keep clear of the whirling sails of his personality. In full career he took no prisoners. He had wounded more by inadvertence than by intent. In fact, his disposition was of the sweetest. Still, like Cassius for Caesar, he was dangerous.

"What brings you to the laboratory, Budd? Are you getting down at last to do some work?" You see what a puritan he transformed me into? I couldn't help myself.

"Nothing so banal, old chap. I came to introduce you to my bride."

"Your *what*!"

"Yes, in spite of all my talk about vice, I have settled all of my accounts around town and am about to subscribe to the narrow confines of matrimony."

"I don't believe it!"

"Doubting Thomas that you are, you shall meet the girl at once. Her name is Mary Maberley. Isn't that perfect: the perfect girl with the perfect name? She is still under age and a Ward in Chancery. But, when it is all settled, she'll have over six hundred a year!"

"But, Budd, how do you intend to marry a Ward in Chancery? There are laws in this country even if you tend to overlook them."

"I'd rather overlook them than look them over, old man. I'll leave that to you. The Act of Union left many inequities behind it for reformers to correct. Blast all laws that put fetters on love! The fact is, Doyle, we are eloping. Yes, we're off on the train to King's Cross tonight. That's why my finding you couldn't wait."

"I begin to see."

"You couldn't help me out, could you, dear fellow? I intend to set up a practice in Plymouth, where my uncle lives. I'll have my brass plaque screwed to a house on a good street before the Lords in Chancery know that Mary is missing. Give us a helping hand, old chap. You know that I am working on a cure for asthma. I'll have hundreds of patients looking to be helped by my elixir, once I've fixed on it. I'll have the loan back to you in no time. Or, better still, when you have your degree, come down to Plymouth and put up your shingle next to mine. We'll have a marvellous time. You'll see. What about it? I'd do the same for you."

I began to give him an argument, the gist of what was

running through my head as he spoke: the education of my
younger sisters and brother, my tuition next term and my
own not inconsiderable debts. But immediately, Budd's face
began to darken. I had seen these squalls before. He would
not brook cattle crossing his track when his horse was at a
full gallop. Before he could give utterance to the unflatter-
ing things he was composing in his mind to say to me,
denunciations, threats, reproaches—he was capable of all or
any of these—I reached into my pocket and brought out my
wallet. Inside I found exactly what I remembered putting
there. Perhaps I had been looking for miracles. I gave Budd
what I could, and before I could season it with a homily on
thrift, he was away out the door and, perhaps, out of my
life. No, the loan was not big enough for that. I was not finished with George Budd. I walked to the door and saw him
sailing down the corridor with a slim young woman cling-
ing to his arm. Just like Budd to forget to introduce us.

When I got back home, a note was waiting for me.
Bridget explained that Dr Bell had sent it round at about
four o'clock. Hastily, I tore it open and read:

> Dear Mr Doyle,
>   Can you come by my rooms after supper? I am
> expecting a visitor at 8:00 pm whom I expect you
> would like to meet as much as I. Bring your notes
> and prepare to make more of them. I suggest
> beforehand that we are in for an interesting
> encounter. Detective-Lieutenant Bryce will have a
> great deal to say, or I miss my guess.
>   Yours,
>   Bell

I walked to the landing and looked at the big clock.
Damn the plodding slowness of the thing!

NINE

For the third time I found myself in Joe Bell's inner sanctum. All was as before except for the coffee tray set out on a folding-table. I also noticed a replenished stock of whisky on a sideboard. The room was already redolent of Turkish shag, the source of which Bell placed upon the arm of his chair, as he reached across to grasp me by the hand.

"My dear fellow, have you heard the news? Half of Scotland is in pursuit of your friend, young Budd. The fool has made off with a Ward in Chancery. He'll end up in Peterhead making fine gravel from granite rocks, and no mistake."

"I saw him this afternoon."

"So, he borrowed money from you as well, did he? Well, it's of no matter now. The chase is well south of here."

"They'll be clapped behind bars, the two of them—just to give them a scare—when they arrive at King's Cross," I said.

"That's why I told them to get off one stop before London. It will give them a fighting chance. It's a fit subject for one of Bab's comic operas."

"Budd's a good fellow at heart. He just..."

At that moment, we heard the outside bell, and in a few moments, Mrs Murchie arrived with a card on a salver. Glancing at it, Bell clasped his intertwined fingers behind his head and asked the housekeeper to show the detective-lieutenant up.

The man who strode into Bell's room was impressive.

His military bearing, his imposing height, the steady look in his clear blue eyes, everything conspired to make the reality live up to expectations. Without quite clicking his heels together, Bryce came to a halt in front of Bell, like an officer reporting to his superior. He did not salute or say "Sir!" but the impression he made suggested that he had.

"I'm so glad you could come, Mr Bryce. Let me introduce my colleague, Conan Doyle. He is a third-year medical student, who runs my out-patients' clinic. It is not an accident that he is here this evening. I invited him to hear what comes of this meeting." Bryce shook my hand, less brutally than he was capable of, and took the chair Bell indicated. Bell, himself, was on his feet and at the sideboard with the whisky decanter. When offered a drink, Bryce declined. Round One to Bryce, I thought.

The policeman sat very straight in his chair, turning to look in the direction of the sideboard. His splendid whiskers valanced a broad, open-seeming face. His eyes were not without humour, but he was used to keeping these and other windows into his character in check.

"Gentlemen," he began, "I came when I got Dr Bell's note, with my curiosity showing, so to speak. I'm looking to learn a good deal this evening."

"Well said, Lieutenant. I dare say that we have the same expectations of you. To that end, let me begin with a serious question: why was young Lambert not released at once when the pawnshop connection was quite exploded by the facts?"

"I see, sir, you have your back teeth set in this thing. Aiblins you should return to your proper pursuits, if you don't mind my saying so."

"Aye, I recognize that tone. It is the noisy sound of officialdom everywhere: 'How may I give the impression of being agreeable and helpful while in fact being neither one nor the other?' Let us all admit, with Mr William S. Gilbert, that 'a policeman's lot is not a happy one,' and get on with it. You are stuck between the Scylla of your superiors and the Charybdis of your own conscience, man. My friend and I have no stake in this matter, no official position. We have been asked by the young man's brother to do what we can. We know about the absurdity of the charge made on the basis of the pawn-ticket."

"It was the suspect's sudden departure from the city, his flight to America that put the wind up. We couldn't ignore that."

"Of course you couldn't. But I would question the words 'sudden' and 'flight' in what you said. In Liverpool Lambert signed his own name at the North-Western Hotel and led you to Cunard's offices. Here again he used his right name."

"There was some haste in the way he settled his affairs here in the city which suggested our further enquiries."

"Aye, Bryce, but you quickly learned that Lambert reserved passage on the steamship before the murder. Just as the brooch was in pawn before the murders."

"I see you have not been idle, Dr Bell." Bell waved away the compliment.

"Sir, I am waiting!" Bell's hawklike face was not wasted on our visitor, nor was the incisive intensity of his eyes. Bryce took a deep breath to allow him time to think.

"Dr Bell and Mr Doyle, it is not the practice of the Edinburgh Police to explain its actions. We have a difficult enough time catching up with the villains out there without giving away our methods. Besides, I was not on the trick until after the man was in custody."

"Lieutenant, you begin to bore me. Your rectitude is admirable. It was never in question. You put forward an enviable defence of the blunders of your superiors. But, sir,

there is a man sitting tonight in a condemned cell waiting
for the hangman. Mr Marwood is bound to arrive at
Waverley Station in two weeks' time. We haven't the liberty to be dainty about the lines of command. As an old
navy man, you should know that."

"How might you be knowing about that, sir?"

"A sailor uses the word 'trick' to mean the spell he has
at the wheel. It is not a police term. I understood the reference and deduce that the term is well known to you. Thus,
the Royal Navy."

"My congratulations. You might put out a shingle as a
consulting detective."

"The suggestion has been made before and more than
once. You have observed a fair introduction to my method:
a combination of observation and inference; science and
instinct. It is a science of trifles. And, am I in form this
evening?"

"Aye, I did a stint as a tar, all right, but I didn't stick it.
This suits me better."

"But, you're not allowed to rock the boat in Edinburgh
any more than in the North Atlantic or off Spithead. Now,
I see you as that rarity among policemen: intelligent and
honest; imaginative and logical. To my way of thinking you
must be frustrated to the point of writing letters to the
Review about this. Don't tell me you haven't considered a
note to the Home Office."

"What do you want of me?"

"You neglected to answer my first question. No matter,
I have others. As a policeman do you believe that there was
a flight from justice? Is there a link between your eye
witnesses and the prisoner? You must have taken down
precognitions. Did the police make all such statements
available to the Lord Advocate? Did the prosecution make
such statements available to the defence? Without such

disclosures, it would be impossible to mount a satisfactory defence. Lastly, who is Webb and why is he marking your footsteps through this investigation?"

At the name, Bryce sat even straighter in his chair than before, if that can be imagined. His right hand began to pull at his earlobe. "Inspector Webb is a colleague. He has had many years of service with the force here and was with the police in Dundee, where he was born, before that."

"He has cautioned the assistant manager at the North-Western Hotel in Liverpool not to show the register. To my way of thinking, he is trying to suppress evidence: the fact that Lambert made no attempt at all to hide his name, the place from which he came or the direction in which he was going. Turn this into the artifice of a desperate man if you can, sir!"

"Gentlemen, I may not stay longer. I thank you both for your courtesy, but you are rowing your jollyboat into restricted waters. I am surprised your bows haven't been stove in yet. But take warning: the fact that it hasn't happened yet does not mean that it will not happen at all. There are interests in this case of which you have no conception. I would heave to, Dr Bell, if you'll pardon another nautical term. Heave to and shove off!"

Bryce was on his feet a moment before my friend. Bryce nodded curtly to each of us and headed for the door. Bell held his ground, saying, as our visitor took hold of the doorknob, "Bryce! Come back, man! You want to see the man executed? Is that it? Will you sleep better knowing that the Corporation of the City of Edinburgh has seen to it that the state has hanged an innocent man rather than have it known that the police foolishly incurred the cost of several trans-Atlantic steamship fares while the real murderer has skipped clean away? Answer me that, man!"

The policeman made no answer. He held himself stiffly

at attention by the door. Bell tried another way. "Lieutenant, come and sit down. These matters are too serious to
trust to our tempers. We are talking about broken necks
not pinched fingers."

"Never, sir! I have said all I intend to say."

"Then I shall have to send for you again."

"And I shall not come."

"I respect your loyalty, your zeal, sir, but—"

"Sir," said the policeman, turning back into the room,
but still holding the door, "be warned. There are others who
know that you are meddling in this business. Your blundering around in Liverpool is well known at the station and
beyond. If you have entertained the idea of spending time in
London for a bit, this might be the moment to put it into
action. Gentlemen, I give you a very good evening."

When the echo of Bryce's footsteps on the stairs had
faded into the shadows along the wainscoting, Bell's comfortable sitting-room felt larger and emptier. "Well," I ventured, "we have been soundly told off! The threat could not
have been put more plainly."

"Is that what you took it for, old chap?"

"In no uncertain terms."

"Nonsense! He was warning us, not threatening us.
Bryce is a man of character. He cannot bring himself to
blab to us while he is wearing his owner's colours. He is not
at liberty to speak, don't you see? I dare say he feels as
keenly about this business as we do, but his hands are tied
by his affiliations. Until he is clear of them, we can look for
no direct help from that quarter. Nevertheless, without
meaning to, he said a good deal that we can make use of
until our next interview with him."

"You heard him say—"

"Not to be taken seriously. When he is convinced that
his masters are not only making errors, but know that they

are making them on purpose, we'll see if our man thinks
again about his allegiances. In the meantime, my dear chap,
there is much to do."

"Where shall we begin?"

"Ah, yes. But of course that follows logically from what
has gone before."

"Sir?"

"I mean, Conan, may I replenish your drink?"

TEN

I did not see my friend the following day. I had lectures to attend and he had classes to meet. At the clinic the next morning, there was no time for private conversation beyond his saying that he had had a very distressful half-hour with the principal of the college. He did not elaborate, but I can imagine that he was threatened with serious action should he continue to pursue this will-o'-the-wisp investigation. The principal and the committees he controlled could move mountains. And in matters of this kind the university was very much a creature of the city. Teachers more celebrated than my friend had come to grief at the hands of these governing bodies of the university after the good burghers began to whisper in their club-rooms.

All of this simply made Bell angry. It did not for a moment wilt his resolve to see justice done to young Lambert. "Tell me, Doyle, who is it who is strong enough to make the police shiver in their boots and dragoon the most powerful men in education to close ranks against me? The answer to that question will be the key to the rest of this thorny question."

On finishing up my day's work, I left the library and walked alone down a narrow street near George IV Bridge. There were no footpaths or curbs. A mossy-green gutter ran down the middle of the cobblestoned way. The street was darkening as the early night settled against the rooftops of the Old Town. Already there was a chill of mid-October in the air, although that was still weeks away.

For some time, I had been aware of a noise behind me.

I was so busy with my thoughts, I hadn't identified it as a coach of some sort. Nor had I noticed that the sound had been growing louder and higher in pitch.

"Look out, ye muckle skellum!"

A four-wheeler was rapidly overtaking me. I could hear the sharp breath of the horses, the sound of the axles running in their hubs. I threw myself into a doorway just as the coach wheels cleaved to the wall, showering sparks from its steel tires, as they rushed past me. By the time I had realized what had happened and climbed to my feet, the four-wheeler was gone up the street and around a bend into the Cowgate.

"Murderers! What were those jolly beggars about? Are you killed or what, young birkie?" I brushed myself off, while the little man with his sharpening stone leaned out from the first floor and looked down on me as I tried to catch my breath. He was dirty to the eyebrows with a bald pate as smooth as a marble bust, but I was never happier to see a human face. I shouted my thanks to him and waved my hat. I looked out into the road. I could see where the base of the walls of the house on my side had been chipped white by the wheels.

"Where are your eyes, you prancing ass? Wandering down the street like kine on a loaning! You must pay up your reckoning, laddie, and the landlord'll leave you be. There are better places to be sore lyin' than in the middle of the road with your head smashed like a football's bladder. This week twelve month a wee bairn was run over where you're standin'. Oh, they run through here like turds through a goose!" The man's homily went on and on and I nodded in time with his cadence until I came to my wits again. I picked up my portfolio of papers and moved off with more care back to the Cowgate.

It would be easy, I thought, in the light of what had

befallen my friend at the university, to ascribe the incident
of the speeding four-wheeler to the invisible enemies Bell
and I had suddenly acquired. No one had ever tried to run
me down before. No one had ever threatened Bell with dis-
cipline either, or so I suspected. My death, quite apart from
the inconvenience to me, would have acted as a further
threat to Bell, an earnest of the seriousness of our antago-
nists. I shuddered as I entered Rutherford's bar. I needed to
have familiar surroundings and faces nearby. I ordered
whisky, which I rarely did, downed it quickly and had
another.

"Well, you 'scaped with the price of a drink. That's
something!" It was Stevenson, of course, like a gypsy baron
in black. He moved his glass from a table to the bar. By the
look of him, as usual, he was several drinks ahead of me.
His head shone with perspiration in the lamplight. I was
amazed that he should so quickly have learned of my accident, then realized what he was talking about.

"I gave George Budd a few pounds to set him on his
way, not the whole of my patrimony, old chap. He seems to
have left you with enough to survive on." While he was
speaking, sometimes swallowing his words, drink making
his tongue thick, he was minutely examining my street-
stained trousers and the scuffs on my shoes. I told him
what had happened near the Cowgate. I omitted to tell him
my guess as to why it had happened.

"Conan, what are you going to do when I am no longer
here to look after you?"

"Louis, what help did you afford me tonight? When are
you off, by the way?"

"I've booked passage on the *Devonia* out of Greenock.
I must be off on Monday. *Ave atque vale*. My parting word
of advice to you, Conan, is this: London is only 396 miles
due south, my friend. Never forget that. Remember what Dr

Johnson said about the high road to London: the sweetest sight a Scotsman ever sees."

"Will Fanny meet you in New York or Boston?"

"I've to cross the continent before I see her fair face. It will be my discovery of America."

"Take a donkey across the mountain passes to San Francisco."

"Oh, Doyle. What a suggestion! Once was quite enough, my friend."

For the remainder of the evening, I quizzed my friend on his knowledge of the social orders of the city. I wanted to know how it worked, which were the leading families, who were the most powerful people. Louis Stevenson was the last person to retain an accurate, scientific picture of what I wanted, but his intuitive, poetic, imaginative impressions were more valuable than a treatise by the Lord Mayor. "Let your memory season this in you, my friend. This town is a sty, a foul cesspool. God, why were we ever born here? It's sure we had no judgment. I say, Conan, that the city is suppurating in its own corruption…"

"But, Louis, be reasonable!"

"We are better educated than the English, but poorer. We have no feeling or traditions for elected office. We all love a laird, we do. All the burghs are tidy blisters of pus, Conan. Government people and administrators are vampires at the throat of a virgin. They're all the same, not one without his arm in the herring barrel."

"I sense your black mood, my friend. You think that travel will cure all ills."

"It will cure mine. I'm selfish enough to be happy with that. But, believe me, Conan, this society eats its young. It will speak all the platitudes of the Good Life, walk to church on Sunday, but let a wee hole develop in the net of their respectability and they'll rival the Huns, Vandals and the Turks with their demonic behaviour until the tear is mended. The first families—and they often as not come out of the law, since we have sold our Parliament to the English—eye one another with suspicion and chalk up their merits every quarter. But let a threat come from outside the sacred borders of Calton Hill and they'll join forces like militia, shoulder to shoulder, to expel the invading vermin. Aye, it's a sorry business. Catch the next train to King's Cross. Leave this stithy of bad dreams. Your hope lies in London, where they don't believe in witches and hobgoblins."

I salted away this sketch in my mind in order to carry the lurid impression back with me to my next meeting with Bell. To find the author of poor Lambert's predicament, we would have to look into areas that are seldom penetrated, corridors of power that enjoy their privileges and guard them jealously.

ELEVEN

The New Gaol, which so intrigued my friend Stevenson when glimpsed from Arthur's Seat, was less picturesque close up. In fact, it was chilling. The massive doors, the recurring themes of stone and iron, the wire-shielded gas lamps fixed high on the corridor walls, the crisp echo of my own footsteps as I was led from the office through a central courtyard to the cells, made a lasting impression upon me. In this cobblestone courtyard, with its echoes of distant clanging of iron on iron, the conducting officer pointed out the portable scaffold resting against a far wall. It was the familiar object of nightmare and penny dreadfuls, larger, perhaps, darker, certainly, but still the old acquaintance of my horrible imaginings.

"That's it!" my guide said proudly, as though he had had some part in inventing it. "She's brand new, this wae-ful woodie, never been used afore. But she'll have a bride-groom before the month is out, sure as weans lap milk." My guide was a well-proportioned, bewhiskered man with a manly, ruddy face that contrasted with his indoor employment. When quizzed about this, he confessed to being an inveterate Saturday fisherman. He did not stay long with the fishing; in another moment he was stomping on the steps of the new gallows, testing their firmness. He returned to me with the following information: "The man from Horncastle has booked a ticket and packed his budget with his wee belts and buckles. Mayhap he's stretchin' a length of rope too. They say he gives a fair drop, does this Marwood. Not like old Calcraft. Now *he* was a throttler

after my own way of thinkin'. He couldna' break a neck at
all if he took the day. With him, there was show enough to
warrant the journey. Now that the job is done behind closed
doors, it's only we warders gets to see. And the friends of
Major Ross, the governor.

"I dinna ken why they fixed those wheels yonder. We
don't pull the woodie out into the street like we did. That's
what they call progress down among the Sassenachs. The
glowrin' crowd've had to do without their hanging-day
frolics, and I don't know that we're all better for it. They
like a proper thrawnin', they do. I enjoy a kick o'heels
m'sel'. They came from all over for the last public hanging.
Near enough ten years agone. You couldna see if you dinna
rent a window view, and that cost more than enough."

I tried but failed to understand why this fellow thought
I might be interested in seeing the gallows, since he was
entrusted by the Head Keeper to show me to the warder of
the condemned cells. Did he expect to elicit some expression of annoyance from me, have me clap him over the
head with my stick perhaps? I pondered the man's character as he led me past rows of iron and stone box-like cells
with dirty hands gripping the bars. The place, for all its
vaunted newness, had the smell of a field hospital in
August.

Dr Bell had got me into this. He suggested that the time
had come to interview our client face to face. Bell directed
me to be his eyes and ears. Just as I had brought the trial to
him, now I was to deliver his client. There were difficulties
in making arrangements, but since Graeme Lambert hurriedly sent word to Alan's solicitor, a successful conclusion
was obtained and thus I found myself being led past the
grim apparatus of death and into the presence of its "bride-
groom."

The condemned cell, as far as I could make out, resembled in most particulars all of the cells that I had walked past on my way thither. Apart from the fact that none of the prisoners in those hundreds of cells would willingly change places with my client, for the advantage of a deal table and a few more square feet of space, the occupant appeared to be indifferent to his surroundings when I first saw him in this setting.

Alan Lambert, his thatch of flaming hair undimmed by circumstances, was staring at the stone floor, or more precisely, the patch of sunlight the high, narrow window let into the tiny chamber. It made a distorted Gothic image which partly ran up the wall. He looked up as the turnkey opened the door.

"Dr Bell?" he asked.

"Much the same: Mr Doyle, his assistant," I confessed, hating to add another disappointment to the others he had had to swallow. I smiled and explained my business. "You must tell me the names and positions of all of the official people you have spoken to since your arrest. Withhold nothing. Any omission may cost you your life."

"I am well aware of my position, Mr Doyle," he said with unexpected heat. "These bars remind me constantly of the shortness of time as well as the vanity of human wishes." After this outburst, he seemed to recover control of his manners at least and offered me the single chair while he remained seated on the slab bed attached to the wall by steel bands.

"I am sorry for the inhospitable welcome, Mr Doyle. I have been acquainted for some time with my brother's account of your activities on my behalf, for which I can never repay you. I have just had an interview with my solicitor, who has informed me that a petition has gone out to the Lord Advocate, who will present it with his recommendations to the Home Office. You know, there is no formal appeal process in Scotland apart from this."

"So I have been informed. The process is slow and inefficient, but in capital cases the Home Secretary gets a hearing. And Disraeli has never been a hanging judge, if I may say so."

"Nor has he been one to interfere with smooth-running institutions. He never reforms a clock that is still ticking. You see, I have become obsessed with time, sir. I can feel it running out on the floor as though from a severed vein."

"You must keep up your spirits, man! Dr Bell is doing everything possible to bring the true state of affairs to the attention of the proper authorities."

"Well said. I must remember to keep my pluck up. But it has already been demonstrated that the proper authorities have no interest in revising their original findings."

"We must make them do that. Remember, the Bard of Avon said: 'Thrice is he armed that has his quarrel just...'"

Again I asked him to tell me the names of the officers and officials who had dealt with him since he was arrested in New York. I marked the names, circumstances and other facts as he remembered them in my notebook. He spoke well of Detective-Lieutenant Bryce, but surprisingly had had few interviews with him. He spoke also of witnesses who had come forward, but whose evidence was not called at the trial. I made note of this as well.

"We are also concerned to learn the names of the people who knew of your intention to leave Edinburgh for America."

"But I told them that months ago, long before the trial!"

"Why were they not called?"

"This is one of the matters I ponder through the night, Mr Doyle. I suspect that my counsel was not informed of their existence. I am to blame. You see, I believed that the case against me was so absurd that the court would quickly discharge me for lack of evidence. Since I knew the charges were false, I thought others would see them in the same light. How could I know that people would invent facts in order to share in the police reward for information?"

"Is that why they did it? There was little enough to share: only two hundred pounds divided among how many? I will tell you how it was divided when I see you again."

"They're weaving the rope, sir, you'd better make haste."

TWELVE

As I walked back through the cell-block to the courtyard, I thought of how the Roman soldiers cast lots for Christ's clothing and parted his garments among them. It was, perhaps, a sentimental similitude—unforgivable in someone of my years and professed religious doubts. Moreover, as Bell would have said had he been privy to my thoughts, they were a waste of time. I had no leisure for romantic comparisons or other unproductive sentimentality.

There was someone standing in the dark doorway leading to the room of the gaol governor. The form was indistinct at first, but the shape moved from the shadows and became the familiar figure of the deputy chief constable. He was enveloped in a dark green ulster against the chill, although the sun made some rash attempts to seek out and warm the dark and rot-filled chinks and crannies along the wall. I decided to be audacious and greeted the man by name: "Mr M'Sween, I believe. A very good morning to you." He regarded me without returning my greeting. I began to feel the awkwardness of my position. He moved towards me, fastening the belt of his flowing coat.

"You would be well advised, Mr Doyle, to make this your last visit to Alan Lambert. You are unwelcome here, sir. You and your colleague are measuring the drop for the prisoner. Have you no' been told that before?"

"Are you speaking of threats from the university authorities levelled at Dr Bell and ruffians in a four-wheeler near the Cowgate? You carry a great staff, Mr M'Sween. Are you so certain you are in the right that you abuse honest folk with your power?"

"When I choose to display my power, Mr Doyle, you will not see it coming. In the meanwhile, I suggest in all friendliness that you desist from aiding and abetting Dr Bell in his contumacy. It will kill him one day. Mark my words." Before I could answer, indeed, before I could begin to form an answer, M'Sween had swept by me and out, through the gate, into the street.

As I crossed the cobblestones of the courtyard, the deputy chief's words hammering on my head, I heard my name pronounced. Shouted, in fact. On finding the source to be a tall, redheaded woman with a striking resemblance to the man I had just left in the condemned cell, I responded with less apprehension than might otherwise have been the case. "Miss Lambert," I called out, "I have just come from your brother." She coloured delicately on being so informally addressed by a stranger, but quickly recovered. She was wearing a tweed skirt and jacket over a taupe blouse with a cameo at her throat, her only artificial embellishment. As she approached I could see more clearly that she had no need of them.

"Indeed, sir, and I am on my way to see him. You left him well?"

"As can be expected," I said in my best medical manner. "He is endeavouring to keep his spirits up."

"It is exactly about that, Mr Doyle, that I wish to speak to you." She stopped a few paces from me and smiled shyly, as though to acknowledge the unusual circumstances of her addressing me on the chance that I was who I was and perhaps to shake off the curse of our doleful surroundings. I was well aware of the sight that greeted her over my shoulder, and made shift to move so that she might see me without seeing the object that dominated the courtyard.

"I am intrigued," I said. "Pray go on."

"Graeme has informed all of us of the work you and Dr Bell have been doing to help Alan. For this you have our deepest thanks. It is a debt we can never repay." I made a motion with my hand to suggest that, even without consulting my friend, payment was the last thing on our minds. She hurried on:

"After consulting Mr Veitch, my brother's counsel, the family wishes to ask you to stop your activities on Alan's behalf." She said it so simply that at first I missed her meaning. I asked her to repeat what she had said, which she did with the same bewildering effect.

"My dear young lady, may I ask you what put such a notion into being? Is this the advice of counsel?"

"I knew you would quiz me about this, although I should have preferred not to be interrogated by you. We have our reasons." In speaking she threw her hands about her ears as though to protect them from my questions. I discovered that I was most disinclined to vex this young woman in any way. I tried to remember whether Graeme had told us what her Christian name was. I recalled from somewhere, from the papers perhaps, that it was Louise. She went on speaking: "Mr Veitch has written to the Lord Advocate and the matter will be reviewed by the Home Office in Westminster."

"I am aware of this, Miss Lambert. But how do our efforts compromise these parallel attempts to save Alan?"

"Sir, we have been informed that the clamour of well-meaning amateurs will only confuse the issue, create factions, turn my poor brother's fate into politics where his life will be made into a rough-and-tumble game for schoolboys. Like a test match! Far better to let Mr Veitch and his friends, who, I am informed, are not without influence, have a clear shot at the goal without encumbrances." She argued with style and pluck. I found that I was quite taken by her manner in spite of the direction her speech was leading.

"I am sorry if your family believes that Dr Bell's efforts
to save Alan from death encumber Mr Veitch's chances. I
shall tell Dr Bell at once. He has already gone to some little trouble—"

"There! I've made you angry. That was the last thing I
wished to do."

"Your brother is facing a deal more than hurt feelings,
Miss Lambert. I wouldn't concern yourself with Dr Bell or
me. It is Alan who will ultimately bear the weight of everything that you do or leave undone."

"I am sorry, Mr Doyle. I put it badly. My father has
quite made up his mind. He has forbidden us to discuss it
outside the family. He will not speak of it further."

"He never approved of Alan before his arrest. Now he
wants to let him die with as little fuss as possible."

"Do you imagine that this has been easy for him? For
any of us?" A blue vein at her temple throbbed with anger.

"Only Alan is faced with the prospect of climbing the
steps to the gallows you are trying so hard not to look at,
Miss Lambert!" Louise Lambert's face coloured. Her hand
touched her breast as she forced herself to see the deadly
machine in the shadows. I took her arm, when I saw her
tremble, but continued my harangue: "When it is over, will
you never question yourself? Will you never ask: Did I do
enough to save him? And what if that answer is 'no,' how
will you live with yourself? How will the inconvenience of
having a hanged felon in the family weigh against the steps
you failed to take to save him?"

"Inveigh against us all you like. You have no conception of my father's need for decorum in all things. He will
even find a way to live this down."

"Ah hah! He has already surrendered Alan to the gibbet."

"Never! He has done no such thing!" Again her hands

covered her ears.

"If I misrepresented him, I am sorry and ask your indul-
gence. But, my dear young lady, this is no time for nice
manners. It seems clear that your father fears that any further fuss on your brother's behalf merely adds insult to
injury. And, I conclude, your father is rather prone to see
injury and insult."

"Mr Doyle, this is all very confusing. Of course we
would like to see Alan spared. Of course we want to do the
right thing. But, are you suggesting that we ignore professional advice? Are you implying that Mr Veitch is part of a
plot to murder my brother?"

"Miss Lambert, in the few days we have spent looking
into the matter, we have discovered gross errors and distor-
tions in the legal process. I am suggesting that you should be
suspicious of anyone having to do with that process. There
is a scandal here in the persecution of your brother. A scandal that no one connected to that system would wish to read
about in the papers. There are reputations at stake, careers,
and what it may lead to I cannot say, but know this: they
will let your brother die rather than let this truth become
known. Oh, when hasn't the state been prepared to sacrifice
an individual to protect the good name of a corrupt system!" I stopped, somewhat overwhelmed by the fury of my
oratory. I had not intended to lecture, or to accuse. I am not
sure what I had hoped to accomplish.

"Mr Doyle, I had no idea … Are you quite well, sir?"
Her eyes were large, blue and luminous and her attention
undivided as she came closer.

"I am sorry, Miss Lambert. You have enough troubles
without my adding to them. You must do, of course, what
you think is right." I was still not sufficiently master of
myself to continue, so I took off my hat and bade the young
woman good morning.

THIRTEEN

Bell was standing in the bow-window looking down into the street, punctuating my tale of the visit to the condemned cell and my unexpected encounter with Miss Lambert with his hearty noiseless laugh as he pulled the roasted chestnuts of significance from the red coals of my narrative. From time to time he touched his fingertips together and sometimes applied them to the windowpane. "This is a singular story, Doyle. Alarums and excursions couldn't be more pointed. If you would like to proceed no further in this business, I would say it was the judgment of a prudent man. As it is, you are borrowing time from your studies well beyond your means. What do you say?"

"And let you see things through to the end? By yourself? If you don't mind my saying so, Dr Bell, you have had better ideas. No, by all means, let the right be done. It may take the two of us to do it."

"I see that the shower of speeches inspired by Miss Lambert has not altogether abated. Would you alter your decision if I told you that this house is being watched?"

"What? I don't believe it!" Bell was looking out the window into the darkness. I got up and rushed to the window. Bell held me back.

"One head at the window indicates very little to a lookout except that the suspect is at home. Two might put the wind up. I like to keep spies where they can be seen. You never know when they might prove useful." Bell returned to the armchair and retrieved his clay pipe from where he had abandoned it some minutes before. When he had cleaned and lighted it afresh, he directed several questions to me about the Lamberts, and other details mentioned at the trial. I spoke for some time, then came to a sudden stop when I remembered the spy across the street. Again, I suggested action. Again, he instructed me.

"Knowing where your enemy is located is almost as good as knowing what to do about him. Mark my words, he will come in handy one day. In the meantime, he is doing us no injury. No, I would be far better occupied if you handed me the third volume of my commonplace books, the one marked 'C.' I found the right volume and passed it across to him. It was a rather messy tome, with pages stuffed in higgledy-piggledy, some attached with pins, some not attached in any way. For a few moments, Bell concentrated on turning the pages to the exclusion of anything else that might be going on in his neighbourhood. I replaced his fallen meerschaum on the table from where it had dropped to the carpet.

"Ah," he said at length, pointing into the book where I could see nothing. "Corry! Montague Corry! That's the man!"

"I beg your pardon?" Bell looked up from the book as though trying to recall the features of the person whose name was recorded in the book.

"Corry is the man to put me in touch with the doctor, the specialist, indeed, who well may be able to cure all of Lambert's woes."

"He must be a remarkable specialist if he has such powers. Who is he?"

"Corry is an old student of mine. I keep a list of them all, you see. You too will have your place. The commonplace books are a record of the men whose careers I have helped. Many, most, in fact, are medical men, but by no means all. Monty Corry is an old friend, but he is not the specialist."

"And this specialist?"

"He is the best specialist in all of Europe," he said. "Yes," he added, "and perhaps the rest of the world to boot. Hand me my portfolio of writing papers. I must think what is best to say."

Once again, Bell became abstracted. I watched him work in silence. He cursed once, taking the page and crushing it in his hands, then straightening out the aborted mess to rescue a line or two for the fair copy he slowly put together. I had seen Bell's crystalline concentration many times before, but this time, he did not, upon completing his work, show me what he had written. He popped it into an envelope and affixed a seal after writing out the address. Since he gave it to me to post, I at least was able to read that much before I consigned it to a pillar box on my way home that night.

The Hon. Montague Corry,
Hughenden Manor,
Near High Wycombe,
Bucks.

FOURTEEN

At the beginning of the week, I stepped into the reading-room of the old free library once more. With the venerable smell of leather and polished wood, it was a change from the dusty and dim medical library where I was bound to meet my contemporaries and be dragged from my books to make an eleventh man for cricket or to kick a ball around in some nearby close for half an hour. Worse were the invitations to a tavern or *howff* nearby. I was most susceptible to such invitations, and, without showing the blue ribbon of a teetotaller, I had to remember that not only had I my studies to manage, but also I must not forget the man in the condemned cell. I understood that he was allowed a portion of beer with his meat; part of the privileges offered to those who were to be legally snuffed out before the month's end.

I was researching everything I could discover about all of the principals in the case: Lambert, Eward and most of all Mlle Hermione Clery. I examined the family backgrounds, the places they visited, what the press had ever said about them until my fingers properly ached with stiffness. My knuckles could easily have chalked a billiard cue. I tried to write with my left hand with slow progress and little success.

"Mr Doyle?" My reverie was arrested by a voice whispering my name. It was more than the conventional decorum of the library that informed the utterance: I detected a special need for privacy.

"Lieutenant Bryce!" for indeed it was he. "How did you find me among so many books? Do sit down. The old fellow beside me will not be back for some time. As you see, he has eclectic tastes: *British Birds*, *Catullus*, *The Holy War*. He won't return from drinking his dinner at M'Cordick's bar for another half-hour at least." The policeman turned to see if his presence in the reading-room had been noticed, but even such a singular occurrence had not been visibly noted. He settled his impressive frame into the chair and moved it closer to mine.

"Mr Doyle, you haven't seen me this morning, nor did I speak aught to you. Do you understand?" I nodded slowly, wondering why he had not picked this same device when I last saw him with Dr Bell. "I have a message for Dr Bell," he said. "Will you oblige me in carrying it to him?"

"Of course, Lieutenant. But what, if I may ask, are you at liberty to say now that you were unable to say in Bell's rooms?"

"I am seeking advice, Mr Doyle. You may have remarked the other night that I was not happy in not being free to help you. My request to Dr Bell has to do with how I might, with honour, achieve that position. Do you follow me?"

"You are seeking a formula that will allow you to speak without incurring the wrath of your superiors."

"In a tidy nutshell, sir. Could you arrange for me to see the doctor at the earliest opportunity?"

"Tonight he is off to give a formal lecture at the Old College. If you could slip in just before he leaves at six-thirty, I'm sure that he will see you." Bryce listened to see if I intended to add more to what I had said, and then rose to his sturdy feet. "I should tell you, Lieutenant Bryce, Dr Bell's house is being watched day and night."

"Thank you, sir. I know something of the matter. That is the reason I followed you here, sir. I believe that Dr Bell has a back entrance. Am I right in thinking that, Mr

Doyle?" I had no expert knowledge of the house, but it was not so very different from my own to make me doubt it. I told him this.

With the slightest of nods to me, he was off again, having chosen to walk to the end of the hall and leave by the main door only after having apparently surveyed the complete reference collection along the walls.

That night, I found my friend in a paroxysm of disorder. All of his drawers were open, several shirts had been taken out and discarded. He was wrestling with a collar button and spoke to me of the virtue of calmness as he fidgeted and fretted.

"You got my note earlier, I hope?"

"Oh, yes. Least of my worries." I had undertaken to fasten his necktie; he lectured me upon the origins of the custom. At last, he was totally assembled in his suit, his papers in good order were placed in a morocco leather case.

"You should have a wee bite to eat before you go," I said.

"I have no stomach for it. Why, oh why do I consent to do these things? Did I imagine that October would never come? How do I look?" he said in despair. I stepped back and looked him up and down. In every way he looked the distinguished academic he was, and I told him so.

At that moment the bell sounded and we soon heard the housekeeper's knock at the door. In less than a minute, Lieutenant Bryce was seated in the basket chair near the fire. Mastering himself for a moment, Bell found Bryce a drink and poured a large one for himself, which, upon second thoughts, he divided in half, giving me the third glass.

"You find me pressed for time, Lieutenant. But what service I may do you is yours if it is within my powers."

"Sir, I have been in the police for thirty years—"

"Oh, we'll never have time if you begin with the story of your life! We know about your medals, your commendations by the chief constable and a' that. Come to the important part."

"Sir, I am going to speak frankly—"

"Certainly, certainly. Why else did you come? There is no one listening in the armoire or behind the door. You may speak to us as though thinking your own thoughts. Only be quick. I have to be gone in less than five minutes."

"Three!" I corrected. "The cab is already at the door."

"A miscarriage of justice has been allowed to occur, sir. I think you know of what I am speaking. I was not part of the original investigation, but by the time they brought me in, they had parted the cable and lost the anchor in this business. They were adrift and couldn't see it! I tried to tell them, but they were caught up in the chase to Liverpool and then to New York."

"Yes, but we've not time for the details now. What do you want?"

"Sir, in the force we know our place. We may not contradict our superiors."

"In the interests of justice, you must speak out, man!"

"That's not the way it's done, sir. It would be like jumpin' into a tank of hungry crocodiles. I would vanish in a flash and young Lambert would be topped on schedule. No, there must be anither way to it."

"Suppose I write to a colleague of mine, Dr Keefer, one of Her Majesty's prison commissioners for Scotland? I will tell him that you need some guarantee of immunity before you will be able to come forward."

"I would need that. And, there's no need for this to become public. No newspaper reporters and—"

"This case has become far too public to guarantee anything along those lines, my friend. There was an editorial in *The Times* this morning. They are highly critical of the way this case has been handled. There's shoulders in the scrum, man, and there are going to be bloody noses before we're done. You can count on that. I will write that wee letter and let you know what happens. Now, I must be off before you. Doyle, have you got my case? Where did I put my hat? Damn it, why do I get myself involved in making public speeches?"

FIFTEEN

Again I found Bell in his rooms after supper. He was reading a medical tome and sipping that excellent port which he from time to time invited me to share. I brought him up to date on the things I had learned from my research.

"You know, that watchdog is still stationed across from your windows, Bell. Do you still believe that he is harmless?"

"Oh, my friend, I never said harmless. But at least we know he is up to no mischief we know nothing of. We have muted him, taken him out of action. But, I see he makes you uneasy. Very well. I will consider what to do about him."

Several days had passed. Busy ones to be sure, but days offering little contact with my friend. With my mother and one of my sisters, I went to visit my father in the nursing hospital. The view from the hilltop establishment was of an impressive reach of the firth, near where it curves towards the city. My father I found hardly altered from when I saw him some weeks earlier. He tried to muster a smile for all of us and kept the conversation well away from the issues that we all were thinking about. He said that he was proud of the progress of my medical studies. He showed me some drawings that he had made in the hospital gardens and I promised to bring him more paper. The experience was enormously exhausting in a way I cannot explain. One owes certain duties to one's parents to be sure, but why is it never easy?

I continued to attend classes, did what was expected of

me in the laboratory, and wrote up some experiments I was
trying in an attempt to master the effects of corrective
lenses on astigmatism.

I had been to see Alan Lambert several times since that
first visit to the New Gaol. We talked at first about the
case, of course. I tried to learn as much as I could about his
movements prior to the crime and immediately afterwards.
After a word with Bell, I prowled the streets and closes near
Howe Street and talked to Lambert's neighbours. Lambert
showed an interest in hearing what I could tell him of these.
I suspect that it helped him pass the time to hear of the
comings and goings of the families on his landing as well as
news of his mistress, Agnes Flett, who now maintained a
room up a stair farther along Howe Street. The condemned
man told me stories laced with good humour, if not keen
observation, about the butcher, the baker and the one-eyed
tailor near Howe Street. In his dim cell, with the gaslight
caged in wire, and the thin blanket folded out of the way at
the end of his cot, he seemed altogether too much fortune's
fool, a plaything of the gods. I found it almost more than I
could bear to keep visions of his fatal appointment with the
hangman from rendering me an impossible guest.

When not in conversation, we played draughts.

"The warders keep me in constant practice," he said. "I
was never a good player, but I am learning. Besides, it helps
to pass the time. I suppose, that's why they encourage it."
It was difficult to look him in the eye, and there was so little else to turn one's attention to in that dusty hole that my
embarrassment was all too clear to my host. He rarely
spoke of the shortening days or of the eight-o'clock walk
on the morning of Thursday, the twenty-third. For the most
part, he encouraged me, and through me Dr Bell, in the
reinvestigation of the crime. Once, he gave way to complete
despair, but quickly mastered himself, and sent me off with

a joke. Whatever happened in the end, I was glad that I had got to know the condemned man.

From what I observed, there was nothing of the murderer about him. He was a fellow from a similar, if slightly more exalted background, but we had much in common. He, and his brother both, had had the heavy cross of his grandfather's still-hallowed name to bear. His achievements had enclosed the family in a cage of propriety which was plainly crushing both of them.

Several times, I met Graeme in the courtyard, either on his way to Alan or just coming from him. He waited for me twice and we walked and talked as we tried to put distance between us and the New Gaol. I introduced him to the barmaids of Rutherford's bar, but discovered that while he had a healthy thirst, he was no Stevenson with the wenches. He told me a little of his life among the painters and artists of the city, of their necessary thrift, their scorn for propriety and their betters. Once, coming from Rutherford's we were overtaken by a group of noisy, well-dressed young men, on a tear of some kind. They were kicking a silk hat in front of them as they lurched and shouted their way along the cobblestones of Drummond Street. It was like a scrum of gentlemen players after a match. With arms flailing and silk scarves flapping about in the wind, they moved on past us. Suddenly, one of the young men turned around and looked back at us.

"There's that ill-skite, Lambert!" he said. Others in his party turned, glaring.

"Say nothing of hemp, Andrew, you'll make him blush."

"Fancy knowing the hangman's coming." This from the fair-haired young man who had lost his hat.

"Come along, man, you'll start him moythering us. They're all the same, the Lamberts! Tarts and clerks, that's their meat! Let's not be thrutchin' up wi' the likes o' them."

We took a stair down into a close and quickly lost ourselves trying to lose our pursuers. The lanes between Drummond Street and Surgeon's Square were sinuous and dark. We heard the young drunks coming after us. From the shadows of a wynd near Infirmary Street, we saw them pass, the moon glinting on their walking-sticks and scarves. In the end, they passed us by and we were able to recover our bearings, but for a time I thought the sound of my own breathing would give us away.

"Young Andrew Burnham," said Graeme. "He was a brute in school. I remember him well. Another was David M'Clung. The one whose hat they were kicking. I knew him at school as well. His father's a director of the bridge company that spanned the Firth o' Tay."

"They were about your age." I said. "Too much money and too much to drink. I don't think they were going to hurt us."

"Andrew Burnham would drown kittens."

We reached the High Street, where we parted. It was easier walking under the street lamps. Still, I suppressed an urge to whistle.

On three of my visits to the New Gaol to see Alan Lambert, I had encountered Louise just coming from her brother. Here too acquaintance blossomed into friendship. One night, she took me with her to her reading-society and we listened while George Meredith read from *The Egoist*, a strange and admirable book, in a small, reedy voice that oddly filled the large hall. She had placed an absolute ban on our discussing Alan's sorry plight and made me agree to abide by it. She kept to her side of the bargain, although I could see when I glanced at her sitting next to me that her mind frequently wandered away from the reading. Afterwards we ate a late supper in the only respectable inn I was

acquainted with, where one ate and talked without danger
to the woman's reputation.

·   "I suppose you think it is all very dashing to be running
about saving people in distress?" she said. She looked at me
as though I were quite ridiculous.

"I haven't saved anyone yet. One gets so little in the
way of help, you see." She frowned and changed the subject. Soon she was describing an amateur play she had
attended with her brother. It kept us from speaking about
what we were thinking about. She went on and on about it.
I listened but with half an ear. She was a dear girl, but quite
firmly under the thumb of her monstrous father.

On another evening, I had the pleasure of her company
at a concert of Handel's music played in one of the assem-
bly rooms close to Princes Street. This was indeed the
evening that took me late to Bell's rooms in Lothian Street,
where I chided him about the lurking sentinel in the bushes
across the street from his house. Perhaps I was overesti-
mating the significance of the dark figure hiding deep in the
shadows. At any rate, as I have said, Bell reassured me. By
now, I was inclined to believe my friend when he asserted
something. And, I must admit, his saying it gave me a night
of happy dreams.

Bell, of course, had written his letter to his friend in the
prison service the evening of his public lecture, but it was
some time before he had an answer. When that arrived, he
mentioned the fact at the clinic and invited me to drop
around for a glass of sherry after my evening meal.

It was not quite eight o'clock when I rang his bell and
was seen up to Bell's rooms by Mrs Murchie, the housekeeper. "Well, sir," said he. "We have our answer from the
Lord Advocate. I've sent a note round to Bryce, with a
word of caution." So saying, he handed me the letter itself
attached to a few lines from his friend in the prison service,

Dr Keefer. The letter from Sir George Currie, the Lord Advocate, read, in part, as follows:

> ... If the constable mentioned in your letter will send me a written statement of the evidence in his possession of which he spoke to Dr Bell, I will give this matter my best consideration ...

"That is wonderful news! I must tell Louise at once!"

"You might also tell Graeme, who, you will remember, brought us into this business in the first place," said he with a twinkle. Then, changing his expression, he added:

"But let me suggest that you do nothing of the kind. For the moment we'll leave simpering Susan and amorous Moll to one side." I was beginning to recognize Bell's moods, but this was a new one.

"You don't look at all happy at this good news. Why?" Bell brought the decanter from the sideboard and poured a glass for me before replenishing his own.

"There is not a word in this about immunity or protection for our friend Bryce."

"Still, it means that they are prepared to listen to him. They can't very well ignore the opinion of such a senior man."

"I feel as you do, Doyle. I know where the nut of right belongs, but I'm not at all assured that it will find its way there by itself. We are thinking of the rights and wrongs of the case; a simple matter of justice. What could be easier? But, the Lord Advocate has other medicine clubs to juggle as well. Remember, he prosecuted Lambert. He must also pass judgment on the virtue of any appeal against his conviction. If wrong has been done, then the Lord Advocate is the cork in the bottle. He will either keep the secret in or he will let it out.

"If we are right, if Bryce is able to explode the case against young Lambert, there will be many red faces in the police. Just imagine the Lord Advocate upon hearing the news that his prosecution has been criticized. It would make for an unquiet house, I tell you. And, you know that the Home Secretary normally seeks and gets advice from the Lord Advocate himself. He is the chief law officer of the Crown north of the Tweed. There is no mechanism for overriding his advice when he, himself, is involved."

"But such expressions of annoyance do them little credit. In their better selves they know that justice must be served."

"Ach, laddie! When I was your age, my head was filled with pretty notions of the right of things. Without shedding my fine notions, I have some experience to put to the other side of it. The chief constable will have allowed a serious error to have been exposed. The error that we detected at the pawnshop must have also been seen by both Bryce and Webb. M'Sween, the deputy chief, must have been informed. Why was the information of the pawnshop and the North-Western Hotel not made known? Why did the men who have uncovered so much crime in the city in the past not correct their bungle and proceed in a new and more profitable direction? There's a question for you to ponder while I'll be refilling my glass."

I did indeed ponder the question and turned up some further questions equally in need of answers. For some reason, this case was not like similar cases. Somehow, the authorities approached it with a difference. Even with kid gloves. What did that mean? There was a potential for embarrassment in the correct solution.

I exchanged my reflections for another dash of wine and received my mentor's approbation. "Capital! Capital!" said he, applauding my efforts by banging upon a silver dish-cover with a slipper. "You should try putting down the details of this case in your notebook, Conan. You might be able to make something in the way of fiction out of it. Certainly, in its first phase at least, it has shown itself to be stranger than fiction."

The bell sounded below, and almost at once Lieutenant Bryce's large form again stood in the open doorway of Bell's sitting-room. "I hope that you have used the utmost caution in coming here, Lieutenant. The house is being watched."

"I was not seen. I came round the back way. I know these lanes, wynds and closes as well as my eyes know the back of my son's wee head."

"Have you come to a decision, Lieutenant Bryce? I told you about my fears."

"I'm out too far to swim back now, sir. I can only go on."

"Splendid! You are a brave man. I have put down a few points which you might include in what you send to Sir George." Here, Bell handed Bryce a sheet of paper, a copy of an original in his hand, which he allowed me to see. For a moment both of his visitors read quietly and then reflected upon the content. In his usually clear hand, Bell had written:

1. Did any witness to the identification on the night of the murders name a person other than Alan Lambert?

2. Were the police aware that such was the case? If so, why was the evidence not forthcoming at the trial?

3. Did Lambert fly from justice?

4. Were the police in possession of information

that Lambert had disclosed his name at the North-Western Hotel, Liverpool, stating where he came from, and that he was travelling to America according to a passage booked some time prior to the murders?

5. Why did the police not abandon the clue of the diamond brooch when it was discovered that it had been in pawn prior to the murders, and that the owner of the pawn-ticket had nothing to do with the theft of some other diamond brooch from one of the murder victims?

"I am sure that you have points of your own that you would like to add to these. But, I think that this list covers the essentials of what we have uncovered."

Bryce lowered the paper in his hand. There was the hint of a smile about his mouth. "What I add, sir, I must keep to myself at present. Such things have to do with breaches of proper police procedures both here and in New York. I might say, also, that there were witnesses interviewed by the investigating officers who were not called at the trial. The significance of these omissions I leave for you to plumb."

"Sir," said my friend, "it is impossible to say now what the result of your action may be. A life, of course, may be saved. A great wrong, righted. But, whatever happens, I know that you have acted with credit to the long tradition of law enforcement in these islands. I would earnestly like to shake your hand. For I believe it belongs to an officer who is both gallant and brave." Here Bell took Bryce's hand in his own two and pressed it warmly. In a moment, moved and at a loss what to say, the policeman had turned and gone through the door. We heard him stumble on the stairs, recover himself and move towards the rear of the house.

When he had gone, Bell looked out the bow-window long enough to satisfy himself that Bryce had used the back lane to make good his escape. At last he turned to me, shaking his head slowly. "I fear that he may yet suffer the fate of those who tell the secrets of the prison house. In cold practical terms, that might mean he'll be turned out of his office, dishonoured and pensionless. A sad fate for a good, honest man. A damnable shame and a black mark against this land."

"But it hasn't happened yet. Perhaps it won't."

"Let's hope you're in the right of it, laddie. Let's hope."

SIXTEEN

It was a week before the hanging. Seven short days remained to young Lambert. Much had happened, but nothing to the good.

Yielding to the demand made privately by Bryce, but independently echoed in the papers, the Lord Advocate, Sir George Currie, appointed Mr Fraser Montgomery, the sheriff of Midlothian, to enquire into the matter and quickly report back to him. What his secret instructions were, we may never know, but *The Times* and *The Scotsman* were quick to point out that the restrictions imposed upon the enquiry were enough to sink it. The proceedings were held in secret. The witnesses, who could not be compelled to come forward, were not examined under oath. The prisoner was not represented, nor was he allowed to attend. The commission was not allowed to enquire into the conduct of the trial. The final blow was this: although, as I have said, the prisoner was not present, the sheriff gratefully acknowledged the assistance he had received from Sir William Burnham, the Procurator-Fiscal, and from Sir Alexander Scobbie, the chief constable of Edinburgh.

It was a disaster. As Bell remarked at the time, "These gentlemen being the officials responsible for the original prosecution, it is not uncharitable to suppose that their interests lay in sustaining the conviction." Indeed, I wrote myself to one of the papers saying: "The police are as much on trial here as Lambert. If the methods of the police are not to be investigated the enquiry is futile." It was a sentiment I had been harbouring for some time. I had often said as much to Bell. This was the first time I had sent in a letter to *The Scotsman* and I must say that it was gratifying to see the result in print.

The chief constable and the Procurator-Fiscal were also gratified when a government White Paper, based upon the commission report, was made public on the 16th. The press, both in Britain and abroad, gave the White Paper a chilly reception. They demanded a reprieve for the condemned man, a new trial. Naturally, questions were asked in the House about what the Home Secretary intended to do about Lambert when it became his problem? The Secretary replied, over much noisy protest from the benches on both sides, that after careful consideration of the whole matter he proposed to do nothing.

Of course, Lieutenant Bryce was destroyed by the White Paper. First, he was suspended from duty at the beginning of the week, before we had seen the contents of the document. He made an immediate appeal to the Lord Advocate, reminding him that he had sent his questions to him with the understanding that the information had been sent at his request and under his protection. There has been no communication from the office of the Lord Advocate up to the time of this writing.

Bell's worst fears had been confirmed, and Lambert was not a whit better off than he had been weeks ago. I climbed the stairs to Bell's rooms with a slow tread that Thursday afternoon, expecting to see a similarly despondent Bell. But, much to my surprise, he was ebullient. His friendly greeting banished my doubts and fears. I must confess he reminded me of the Act Five Macbeth: doomed, but making a good end, "At least we'll die with harness on our back."

"Is there nothing we can do?" I asked. "I feel so helpless."

"There is a good deal. Now that the constabulary is
showing Bryce its abundant power, Bryce may no longer feel
bound to keep his counsel on the case. He may now tell us
what we might never have learned." There was a brightness
in Bell's cheeks that did not sort well with our situation. I
suspected that he was less distraught than I was. Under it
all, Bell was enjoying himself.

"Conan, we have been busy these last few weeks trying
to free an innocent man. All of our efforts were bent on
demonstrating the foolishness of Lambert's arrest and prosecution. Now, that approach must be abandoned, or at
least buttressed by another. We must now concentrate on
discovering the identity of the real murderer."

"How will that help poor Alan Lambert? He will be
safely dead in a few days. Any discovery we make about
the true killer will be of no practical use to him. Shouldn't
we press on with our first approach while there is still
time?"

"We are meeting with Bryce at Waverley Market
in forty minutes. We will see what he has to say for
himself."

"Aye, but…"

"But what, Doyle? You must not admit despair. There
are seven days left, remember, one hundred and sixty-eight
hours. Mountains can be moved in half that time."

"I am afraid that we will still be too late. The best we
may hope for is to clear the name of a man unjustly
executed."

"Nonsense! We may have to resort to kidnapping Mr
Marwood, but I doubt if it will come to that. Take heart.
There's many a shaw and glen twixt where we are and
where we would be, but I think I know the way. With your
help, I think we will have a great success."

In half an hour, we were wandering among the barrows

and stalls of Waverley Market. Freshly killed meat hung
from hooks on iron stanchions. Butchers were selling off
the cuts as they came to them: legs before ribs, shoulders
before the scrag end of neck, which was the last to go. Coils
of fresh and smoked sausages festooned stalls dealing in
preserved meats, hams, trotters, and sides and collops of
bacon. Some brownish kale was to be seen along with
beets, carrots, turnips, potatoes, parsnips. The quality was
not good, but at this time of the year frosts had already
killed much of what was in the ground. In addition to the
vegetable and meat vendors, various craftsmen plied their
trades: makers of sporrans, spoons made of horn, purses
and bagpipes; cobblers; harness-makers; coppersmiths
banging out kettles and porridge pots, making a great
racket with their mallets on the yielding metal. Underfoot,
one trod on the litter of the morning's business, including
the horseballs left behind by the carters' horses. Above the
sharp smells for the nose and a cornucopia of produce for
the eye, there was everywhere a cacophony of shouts,
curses and cries from the vendors. Bell bought a few pence
worth of apples of a dusky, greyish tinge. I comforted
myself with a lump of candy rock.

Against the wall of the railway station, using that wall
as a support for this much more flimsy structure, a tearoom
beckoned. It offered a substantial breakfast for the vendors
and their customers, who sat on joint stools with their
elbows on small white deal tables. Against a back wall, a
heavily built but comely lass was cooking fresh herring,
bacon and toast over an iron stove, which was vented by a
pipe going through the roof. When she wasn't putting more
wood to the fire, she was refilling cups of strong black tea
and more or less keeping up with the demand. Apart from
a little slavey carrying in wood and trying to clear the
vacated tables, I could see no one else running the shop.

The cook, whose face shone with the work she was doing, carried a heavy sporran on a wide leather belt around her waist, which incidentally kirtled up her skirts becomingly. Into this she put the pennies her customers paid, all the while keeping up a spirited banter with the salty lot of regulars.

We had not been seated long in the tearoom, when I saw Bryce sitting at a table in the back. He was nursing a stoneware mug between his large hands and breathing in the steam. Bell gave no sign that he had seen the suspended policeman, rather he slowly scanned the tearoom looking for spies. Satisfied that neither we nor Bryce had been followed, he picked up our own steaming mugs and made his way among the tables, crammed with stall operators, to the back wall. Bryce made an indication that he was about to rise, but in the end did not.

"Lieutenant Bryce, I am glad you consented to see me again. As you know, time is of the essence."

"Doctor, I hope that you and your friend will address me no longer according to my rank on the force. In the navy, I was a chief petty officer. I see no harm in your calling me 'chief,' if you wish."

"I would like to think, Chief," said I, "that you will soon be restored to your former rank. Indeed, if we are able to save Lambert, you may look for better." When I finished speaking, Bryce looked at Bell, who slowly shook his head back and forth.

"You're but young yet, Conan. It is hard at your stage of life to recognize the fact that an organized group, like the army or the police, has a sense of itself that far exceeds the vanity of a single man. The force would rather serve our friend roasted as a Christmas goose than admit that he had the right end of the stick all the time. People are fallible and make errors, organizations never. That is true generally the world over, but never more vindictively than here in Edinburgh."

"You have the right of it, sir. And I canna be blaming you for my predicament. I made this berth long ago. Now I must lie in it." Bryce saw the interest in our faces and went on to explain.

"Years ago, in 1875, a young Canadian named Sennett was arrested for the murder of a Mrs M'Nabb, an elderly recluse, who kept in her house a fortune in gems. No less than a dozen eye witnesses came forward and swore that they recognized the young man as the murderer escaping the scene of the crime. The young man protested. The witnesses claimed their share of the one-hundred-pound reward. I discovered that, in spite of the solid case being built against the man—by now there were over one hundred who swore in their precognitions, or statements, that Sennett was the man—there was something to his story that he was not even in Scotland at the time of the woman's death. The man was living rough, so it was hard to prove anything, but then he remembered that he had pawned a waistcoat in Antwerp for a franc or two. I went to Antwerp, found the pawn-ticket with the accused's name on it. It was dated the day *after* the murder. Did I get a medal? Was I mentioned in despatches? No! I had cheated them of a first-class sensational murder trial. My days on the force were numbered from that time."

"It certainly tells a cautionary tale about dealing with witnesses who claim to have seen the murderer when what they see most clearly is a substantial reward that has been offered for information."

"Are you suggesting," I asked in all naïvety, "that people will willingly perjure themselves and send a man to the gallows for a few guineas? This is a sad comment on this country."

"On humanity," corrected Bryce with a look at Bell.

"This is a moving tale, Chief, but its lesson only confirms what we have just told our friend here. Let's move to more practical matters. What are you now willing to tell us that your former position made impossible?"

"There are several items. First, witnesses were shown photographs of the accused before they made their identifications. They simply picked out the man who resembled the photographs. In New York, the witnesses saw the prisoner in custody prior to making their identifications."

"This is abominable! Very doubtful practice in law, but, I doubt whether it is strong enough to stop the execution."

"Witnesses saw the prisoner in various places near his flat both before and after the time of the crime. The only witnesses called were those most easily discredited: Lambert's mistress and his servant. Further, there were trial errors: the Lord Advocate spoke of things as though they had been entered in evidence, which were in fact only mentioned in his own opening remarks, saying that he *intended* to enter them in evidence. To make matters worse, the judge, in summing up, aggravated this error: he too was prepared to believe that saying a thing was in evidence was the same as having it in the record."

"Yes, I remember noting that in Doyle's excellent summary of the proceedings. But, it won't help us if we simply make the Lord Advocate and the judge look like ninnies. We need a major flaw in the case."

"The Lord Advocate said that 'we know nothing about the man's movements from six o'clock to a quarter to ten that night.' In fact, he was seen by several independent witnesses close to his flat in Howe Street during that time. Is that good enough, Dr Bell?"

"It's good, but not good enough. I'm looking for better. Can you find it?"

"The maid, Hélène André, stated once that she did not see the face of the murderer, because he was walking away from her. To Mlle Clery's agent she said that she did see his face and that the man was known to her. More about that later."

"Ah-ha! Now we are getting some place! That would account for the curious incident of the door."

"What curious incident?" I asked. "The door has not figured in this investigation in any way."

"That is the curious incident," Bell said. "In all the talk of robbery, we have seen no sign of a forced entry. How is that possible when the door is heavily locked from the inside? There are only three ways that the door could have been opened: the door was left open and this accidentally coincided with the arrival of the assassin, which seems highly unlikely; the murderer had his own keys; or one of the victims opened the door and let the murderer into the flat. There is no other way. The maid may have left the door unbolted when she went out, but there were two spring locks, which would have kept an intruder powerless unless he had brought with him a battering ram.

"This explanation makes excellent sense in the light of a robbery that took nothing from the flat. Only the diamond brooch was missing from the jewel box in Mlle Clery's bedroom. A bagatelle among so many riches. I suspect the maid might have been made to account for that loss if her belongings had been searched. Too late now, of course.

"Only two things were taken from the flat that night. Two precious and irreplaceable items."

"If you rule out the missing brooch, Doctor, to what do you allude?"

"I allude simply to the lives of the victims. The murders were not by-blows, the frantic act of a desperate criminal in pursuit of valuable property. No! The murders were an end in themselves."

"But to what purpose?" I demanded. "Mlle Clery was universally loved and admired."

"That is so. Nevertheless…"

"Dr Bell," said Bryce. "You may well be right. But how do you propose to prove it in seven days?"

"As you say, it may tax my skill to the breaking point. But that may never be put to the test."

"Why?" I asked.

"We have another and perhaps more serious problem."

"Which is?" Here both Bryce and I spoke together.

"If you look at the door to the tearoom, you will see the sweating face and sturdy trunk of Inspector Webb standing with four constables. I don't imagine that they are here to taste the oatcakes."

"What are we to do?"

"That is a very good question!"

SEVENTEEN

With my back to the entrance, it was difficult for me to turn to confirm what Bell had said without giving notice that the policemen had been discovered. I saw all I needed in the eyes of my companions. I repeated my question about what we were to do and again got no very clear answer.

"I suspect that they will not bother us as long as we appear to be engaged in talk. I suggest that we continue," said Bell. "You said earlier, my friend, that the maid said some startling things. I wonder if, when I return, you will tell us about them." Here Bell slowly got to his feet and walked over to the stove, temporarily abandoned by the cook, who was haranguing a customer about a bad copper. Bell very deliberately, but without any quick or awkward motions, moved the toast rack over the blazing stove lids. Next, he threw some confectioner's sugar, which stood conveniently nearby in a brown earthenware bowl, on another stove lid. Just as slowly as he had gone, he returned to us.

"Joe...?"

"Dinna fash your mind about it, Conan. I have merely prepared for our hurried departure. But it will not ripen for some moments. Meanwhile, Bryce, pray continue."

"The maid, Hélène André, spoke to Mlle Clery's agent, a man named Tom Prentice, in nearby Canning Street on the night of the murder. When he was questioned, he told the officers that the woman told him that she did indeed see the visitor's face and that she recognized it as being 'like,' she said 'like,' a man she knew. The officers took down that name and reported it to their superiors."

Slowly, as we talked, a fine mist of smoke was building up around the stove. With the pipe and cigarette smoke already filling the room, nobody noticed. But I could see a thicker cloud of denser smoke developing from the burning sugar. Meanwhile, Bryce continued his story.

"Who that man was, we do not know. Nor do we know what he said to the officers when, in turn, he was called upon to make a precognition. In all the reports referring to this gentleman, the name never appears; in its place the initials 'XYZ' are used. When I was brought into the case I was told to inform Tom Prentice that his statement about XYZ had been looked into and that there was no point in that line of inquiry. XYZ had satisfied the investigating officers and no point would be served by proceeding further in that direction. Of course, by that time, the chase had moved on to young Lambert, who had sailed to New York in what was then seen as undue haste."

"Where is Tom Prentice now?" I asked, thinking that perhaps he might be encouraged to identify Mr XYZ.

"He returned to New York as soon as the trial was over. He runs an artists' management agency on Fifth Avenue."

"Doyle is right. We should cable him at once. There is no time to waste."

The smoke in the tearoom had now become impressive. I was not afraid to turn to look at the door, for I could hardly see half the distance with any clarity.

"Gentlemen," Bell announced, getting to his feet and placing a few coins on a saucer, "I believe the time has come to make our departure. Come." Without showing the least awkwardness, Bell moved smoothly through the tables to a small door against the east wall of the tearoom. It opened easily, once a crate of fresh herring had been

moved away from it. We had followed Bell at a sufficient
distance so as not to tread on his heels. Bryce was ahead of
me and through the door before me. The small landing led
to a flight of steep stairs which were wide enough for one
person at a time. When I saw them first, Bell was nearing
the top, with Bryce somewhere in the middle. I closed the
door behind me, sighting through the glass a room now
overwhelmed with smoke. People were on their feet and
rushing towards the main entrance. Webb and his escort
moved through the smoke, while the cook swatted the
smoke with her apron. Bell opened a door at the top of the
steps and I hurried to catch up.

We were on the roof of Waverley Station. Unlike the
stations in London and elsewhere, where curved iron
arches held up a large area of glazed roof, the Edinburgh
station rejoiced in a flat roof, enlivened from time to time
with ridges of inverted V-shaped walls of windows which
brought light into the structure while keeping the weather
at bay. I was still blinking in the daylight, when Bryce
grabbed my arm and hurried me with him behind Bell's
rapidly disappearing back. He was headed along the rim of
the roof, where it overhung the market, and moving in a
westerly direction against the wind. Looking back over my
shoulder, I saw Inspector Webb just coming through the
door to the roof. At his heels his posse of four came cough-
ing into the air. Webb quickly picked a path along the edge
of the roof and closed the distance between us. Bryce, who
was ahead of me, saw this and moved past me towards our
pursuers. Without preamble, he clashed with Webb on the
very lip of the roof. They grappled like urchins in the market below, each taking and giving advantage as they strug-
gled. In a moment they were rolling near the edge, still
clasped in one another's strongest grips. Bryce's leg hung
for a time suspended over empty space, but he righted

himself, got to his knees and was soon coming after me
again. Webb's minions had caught up by this time, and
were able to assist their chief, whose foot had somehow
gone through the roof and made his leg prisoner almost to
the kneecap.

I saw all this as I ran, as though my life depended upon
it, after Bell who was still a short distance in front of me.
Soon we came to Waverley Bridge, which spanned a dozen
railway lines that vanished under the bridge and into the
station. Towards the middle of the station roof, coinciding
with a supporting arch of the bridge, a colony of gulls took
to the air. Through the froth of feathers in movement, I saw
what Bell was heading towards: a ladder which led from
the station roof to the bridge railing. Without turning
around, Bell reached up and grabbed the highest rung and
quickly scrambled up the black, and, as I found a moment
later, none too solidly anchored, iron ladder. Bell's feet rang
on the rungs like reports of gunfire in a belfry. Fragments
of rust and paint floated down upon us so that it was necessary to avert our eyes from the scrambling form above us.
On reaching the top, he climbed over the railing onto the
pavement of the bridge, heavy with its daily round of carts,
drays, carriages and omnibuses. In less time than it takes to
describe it, we made the same ascent and joined him on the
sidewalk. Limping, Webb had not yet reached the foot of
the ladder.

"I think that it might be useful if we lost ourselves in
the university for an hour. What say you, Doyle? Do you
think you can seek out some congenial prospect out of the
wind?" My first thought was to lead them to Rutherford's
bar, but at this hour it would have been a noisy hive of students with more money in their purses than sense of what
to do with it. (You see, my Catholic upbringing had not
made me proof from Calvinist judgments. Here in Auld

Reekie these sentiments are imbibed with our mothers' milk.)

Bryce had hailed a four-wheeler and we quickly packed ourselves inside. I gave the driver an address on South Bridge Street, which was close both to Bell's house and to Drummond Street in case we wanted Rutherford's after all. I felt my face wet with perspiration. Bryce's face was shining with his exertions as well. Only Bell, who never did a stroke of exercise as far as I knew, remained cool. His breathing was calm and unhurried, unlike Bryce and me, who were puffing like a pair of grampuses. Bell leaned his head back on the headrest of the cab and closed his eyes as though a flight from the police was a common pastime with him.

It was not a long ride, just a medium run down Cockburn Street, then along the Cowgate a short distance to South Bridge. The university looked busy enough to intimidate all policemen. Before the cab came to a stop, scraping its wheels against the curbstones, Bell, without opening his eyes, demanded of Bryce:

"Who else, besides Prentice and Hélène André, knows the identity of XYZ?"

"Constables Weir and Douglas took the precognitions. Weir is retired now in Gairloch, where his people come from. Angus Douglas is in charge of the wee stationhouse in Thurso, near John o'Groats."

"Both conveniently remote."

"Aye, and neither will say aught M'Sween hasn't authorized."

"As I suspected. Go on."

"Webb had access to the original precognitions. All I saw were copies with the pseudonym and an epidemic of asterisks showing where part of the statement had been omitted in making the copies."

"Who else saw the original?"

"Webb's immediate chief, M'Sween, the deputy chief constable."

"Who else?"

"The Procurator-Fiscal, Sir William Burnham."

"How that name keeps popping up, young Doyle. Do you detect a pattern here?" I delayed my response as we climbed out of the four-wheeler and sorted ourselves out again on the sidewalk.

"It would seem, sir, that as head of the whole process, the man who had to determine whether it was murder or not, his name was bound to be attached to statements at the highest level."

"As a layman," Bell said without feigned modesty, "I would accept that as accurate. But what do we know? Another thing, are other precognitions normally subject to this sort of censorship, Bryce?"

"No, Doctor. I have seen everything else. Only this was withheld."

"So! Our Mr XYZ may demand to be handled with kid gloves. The affair between Mlle Clery and Mr Eward may become fodder for the press, but Mr XYZ is well above such discourtesy. Not only is his name shrouded in secrecy even in official private police reports, but you, Bryce, are sent out to tell the witness who originally brought the name up to forget the whole business."

"It smells like a month-old kipper to me," said Bryce.

"It smacks of tampering with the truth at a high level," I added.

"I agree with you both. A very pocky business. The question is: what are we going to do about it?"

EIGHTEEN

Bell cabled Tom Prentice at his talent agency in New York from the trans-Atlantic cable office in Bank Street. That was our outside chance. From the safety of America, he might be willing to send the name he had been encouraged to forget. But we did not have the luxury of waiting for the answer. Bell began hammering Bryce with questions about Inspector Webb. As the other person who knew the identity of XYZ, he moved to the centre of our enquiry. It did not escape Bell's notice that we were now in search of the man who had only a few minutes ago tried to find us in the market tearoom. "The detective detected," he muttered as Bryce tried to recall what he knew of the man. We both looked at Bryce.

"Webb is a man who has been walking on my shadow for the past fifteen years. He has been studying my methods. I never liked the man, although I've tried. He refuses to use the sense he was born with. He's always trying to think of the answers he gives in political terms: what is the answer they want to hear? He is a fellow who makes Uriah Heep look like a good, matey sort, if you know what I mean. Robbie Webb is..." He stopped, then continued after a moment for reflection: "a *good* policeman by most standards. He's dogged, thorough and clever. Bristol fashion all round. But, as I said, he follows orders. When Keir M'Sween orders Webb to soop, Webb will find a broom and soop. He will find out what the deputy chief wants to know. He will find evidence that I murdered Mlle Clery if that's what M'Sween sends him out to find."

"His name is Robert Webb? I know something of the man," said Bell. "His home was near Dundee, I believe. I remember that he served on the police force there."

"Yes, Robert Fergus Webb, born in Dundee, son of the town drunkard. He set out to better himself and did so. I don't think he ever forgot his origins, nor forgave them."

"If he was trying to arrest us at the market an hour ago, what time will he finish his shift today, Bryce?"

"Unless he has an appointment which will take him away from the station or he has been ordered to work a double shift, he will finish at six o'clock. He lives in one of the lands in a close off Richmond Lane. One of the old tenements."

"Tonight, I mean to pay him a visit."

"You will never get him to say a word, Dr Bell."

"Lieutenant Bryce, you may not remember, but when you came to see Doyle and me the first time, you said many things that you didn't mean to say. Everybody does. Unless I find him gagged, he will undoubtedly tell me something of value."

We parted in the small museum, near the Etruscan antiquities, after Bryce had given me Webb's address hurriedly written on the margin of his newspaper. "Will you not come with us?" asked Bell.

"It's a broken sea, Dr Bell, and I have no desire of broaching-to with our friend Webb. You have no history with the man. You'll do better without me." With that, he nodded farewell and loped off down the wide steps. Before we parted, Bell gave me instructions to meet him at six o'clock at a place we both knew in a close behind the City Chambers.

In a short time, I had walked to the free library. On entering the reading-room, I was annoyed to find that the place at my accustomed table was occupied. My pique turned to joy as I recognized the form of Louise Lambert. She was reading an atlas illustrating our most recent discoveries concerning the lakes of central Africa. By that token, I guessed that she had not been waiting long. I had told her that I could often be found there, and once she had accompanied me to the very table.

"Miss Lambert!" I said, in some surprise.

"Mr Doyle, I have been waiting for you. I hope—"

"I am delighted to see you." She closed the tome and looked up at me, turning in her chair and creating a delightful effect with her chin raised on a flawless neck: like some splendid crane from the plashy brinks of those distant equatorial lakes.

"I must talk to you, Conan. May I use your Christian name?"

"Of course. Tell me, tell me."

"I can no longer keep to my father's instructions. There is too much at stake and time is slipping by."

"Yes."

"When we last spoke about Alan, I told you what my father intended me to say to you should we meet. As a dutiful daughter, I played my part. I told you to stop trying to help Alan, lest that well-intended interference spoil the few chances that might save my poor brother."

"Of course, I remember very well."

"I spoke to you as I was instructed. You have not heard from me. Dare I speak my mind to you?" I nodded, holding my breath. What a lovely thing she was, with her head lifted, her face catching the light from the high windows. "Please, Conan, please, do not confuse me with the sentiments of which I have been the unwilling messenger."

"But, Louise, you mustn't think for a moment that we paid attention to what your father wanted. Bell saw through that at once." For a moment, Louise looked shocked. Then she peered at me very closely.

"You mean, you saw through the stratagem? Was I as

transparent as glass?"

"By no means. We were determined to prosecute our investigation despite all opposition. Your father's wishes played no part in our plans. Alan was our only object. If we can save him, we will."

"If you can save him, you must!"

"Yes, let justice be done…"

"Though the heavens fall!"

That night at ten minutes after six, Bell and I found ourselves sitting in a *howff* called The Last Minst. The rest of the sign, the "rel," had rusted away, but the nod at the memory of Sir Walter was noted. It was a smallish corner room with yellowish light from a lamp on the wooden bar. The lamp made a hissing sound, like the sound of a malevolent insect. The landlord was unshaven and dirty, but his establishment gave us an excellent view of the entrance to the tenement in which Webb lived his solitary life.

When I came in, Bell greeted me with news that astonished me: Inspector Webb had sent a message round to his rooms stating that he wanted to speak with Bell. Bell answered the note—it came by messenger—agreeing to meet him the following morning at seven forty-five in a tavern close to the market where we had had our run across the rooftops.

"If that is the case, why are we waiting here?" I asked.

"Why, to see Webb, of course. I have no intention of meeting him tomorrow, even if he comes alone. No, this suits us better."

We tasted the beer, or, to be more accurate, we sat with a pewter mug of it before us. On trying the contents, Bell grimaced and set the container down on the table again with a smack that echoed his critical judgment. Without being quite as dramatic, I rejected my drink as well. As far as the landlord was concerned, our rejections touched him not; he was equally indifferent to our approbation and our abuse. Joe called out for a better-known ale, which duly arrived at our table. While drinking and chatting about inconsequential matters, we kept our eyes on the doorway to the staircase leading to Inspector Webb's flat. We watched a woman carrying washing leave the tenement and we watched her return half an hour later. Meanwhile, others came and went: a man in uniform, an ensign in the navy; several women, painted for a night on the town; a tall, veiled widow of a certain age making slow progress with a furled umbrella; a bearded man wearing a plaid over his shoulder, like a rural dominie fallen on hard times—Bell put him in Perthshire from evidence he did not make clear; and sundry others, none of them entirely disreputable, but neither were they the *crème de la crème.*

After a wait of more than an hour, it appeared that our guess that Webb would return to his lodgings when he had completed his shift at the station was ill-founded. We decided to give up our vigil and seek him out elsewhere. For my part, always happy to have a sow's ear when a silk purse is denied me, I suggested that we climb the stairs to his rooms just to see where our quarry lived and more accurately gauge the sort of life he led. Together we left The Last Minst and crossed the close to the tenement we had been observing. The turnpike, or corkscrew stairs, wound their dark way in circular fashion up the inside of a round towerlike projection from the house proper. Bell lit a bull's-eye lamp and shone light where it may never have penetrated before. It was one of the old lands, dirty, damp, cold and in need of repair. The steps wanted sweeping. All sorts of offal and garbage had fallen on the flagstones and simply been left there to rot or become part of the dust that held the cut ashlar stones together.

On each door, we looked for some sign as to the

occupant. Many of the doors were unmarked. Halfway up, Bell accosted a young woman, with a child in a basket, on her way out. He addressed her as politely as though she were the Queen of the Night:

"My dear young woman, my friend and I are seeking the flat of Inspector Webb of the police, who lives here, I believe. Can you help us? As a stranger in Edinburgh yourself, you'll appreciate our difficulty. It's a far cry to Tarbert, my lass."

"How'd you ken I'm from Lewis? And who are you with your questions like some catechist come to bedevil me with more pernickety troubles, when, God knows, I have enough of them already?"

"Your shoes are country made, lass. And your fine skirt was woven, then sewn, in a cottage, I'm sure. There's no mistaking the craftmanship of the Hebrides. Even the baskets tell their tales. And a fine-looking laddie you have, Missus."

"Craftsmanship is it? I took this off the loom myself not ten weeks ago in Balallan. What are you, some kind of fortune-teller?"

"Ah, my dear young woman, I wish I were. But, you see, we come asking for directions. Do you know this Inspector Webb at all?"

"Know him? I wish I dinna. He harps on wee Ruaridh's bawlin' o' nights. The bairn's a wee bit wabbit with the teeth comin' in just now. And wasn't he a wean h'self once, I'm askin'? And h'self's no' that secret, mind. He's been stumpin' and shoutin' somethin' awful not an hour agone."

"If this is your door, then he must be your neighbour. Is he one up or one below, since there's but one flat on each landing?"

"You'll have to climb up one more round on the turnpike, sirs. And give the gentleman no good word from me, if you please." She ran off with her basket and baby as lightly as young feet could carry her. We climbed the few remaining steps to the next door. Bell rapped with his gloved hand and waited. There was no answer. He knocked again.

"He may have had meetings or appointments outside his office work," I suggested, just as Bell tried his door. "I myself would not hurry back here unless compelled to do so. The neighbourhood—" I didn't finish what I was about to say because the door swung inwards at Bell's touch.

They were Webb's rooms sure enough. An old uniform was hanging on a peg by a window which overlooked the close we had been watching. In this room, it appeared, Webb made simple meals for himself with water carried up the turnpike, and slops sent into the street from the window shortly after the warning cry: "Gardeyloo!" He was not a tidy person, the grease marks on the wall made me imagine his collars, cuffs and the shine on his boots. The stove was filthy: one could reconstitute his last hundred meals from the evidence on the floor.

"Perhaps we should leave and come again," I suggested. My non-existent Calvinist ancestors were already warning me of footsteps on the stairs.

"We found the door open, Doyle. We are simply having a look around in case a robbery has been committed. See if any valuables have been taken from those drawers." Bell went into the next room, which was almost completely filled with a brass bed. The worn ticking of the mattress gave further testimony to Webb's housewifery. I hurt my knee painfully as I peered under the bed. I had kneeled on a black umbrella that had fallen to the floor. Beneath the bed I found only the expected slut's wool and the odd sock. In some pain, I threw the umbrella on the bed, and checked my wound. It would serve, as Mercutio says. Next to the bedside table, I saw a Thornton-Picard camera with its tripod. The camera was curious in that a dummy lens had been inserted in front. The true lens was fixed to the left-hand side of the box, disguised as a focal plane shutter adjuster knob. I imagined that the interior would reveal an arrangement of mirrors. On a table, several exposed glass plates were assembled in a series. Bell picked one of them up, tilted it at an angle to his torch, then studied it in the oblique light.

"Hello!" he said. "Here is a likeness of you, Doyle, coming from the Parliament House." He handed it to me most carefully by the edges. I held the glass to the light and recognized a negative image, which with some manipulation of the plate became myself coming from a session of the trial.

"Interesting," said Bell. "Very interesting." I replaced the negative where it belonged and cocked an eyebrow in the direction of my friend.

"Why so very interesting?" I asked.

"This case becomes more and more fascinating as time goes on," he said. "This image of you at the trial, for instance, can be dated with a good deal of accuracy."

"That's right. The trial was over a little more than a week after we agreed to help Lambert."

"Exactly! You see, that was before we questioned the pawnbroker; before we went to Liverpool!"

"Before the authorities could have had any idea that we had taken an interest in Lambert's affairs. I see!"

"Yes. It is curious, isn't it? Someone close to Lambert must have told the police to be on the lookout for us. How careless it is to imagine that one is invisible. We were well over our heads in this business when we thought we were simply testing the water."

"But who could that have been? Alan and Graeme are above suspicion. And I will vouch for Louise."

"I thought you might," Bell said with a smile. "Whom

does that leave? Who tried once already to dissuade us from taking a role?"

"The old man! Lambert, *père*!"

"Precisely. He has been working against his son's interests from the beginning. No! That isn't exactly right. He has been working against us, to be sure, but he may be persuaded that we are not helping Alan's cause. He may have had assurances from a source promising redress from a completely different direction. Assurances that may carry provisions that Lambert and his family do not stir themselves or take steps independently."

"Put like that, it is plausible. What can we do about it?"

"I have the glimmerings of an idea, Doyle. But, that will have to await our return from this dismal hole."

Before leaving the flat, Bell and I tried the remaining drawers in the dresser and all other crannies. I turned up a penny dreadful with a lurid illustration of the final end of Sweeney Todd, the Demon Barber. Pressed between the pages was the following written on a scrap of paper:

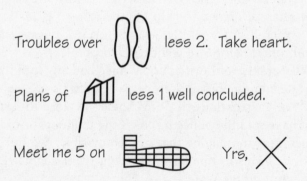

"What on earth...!" I began. Bell snatched it from me and held the paper up to the light.

"Good paper. Watermark suggests a well-to-do author. And these symbols are not altogether unknown to me. But, I will have to remember where I first saw them. I recall it was while I was engaged in researching something else. All I have to do is retrace my steps." He made a quick sketch of the note and pocketed it. The original, he replaced facing the engraving of Sweeney Todd *in extremis*.

Bell and I walked out onto the landing, then paused. Without a word to me, he turned and re-entered the empty rooms. "There is something peculiar about the bulge in the wall by the window, Doyle. It suggests some external architectural feature, which I do not remember seeing when I examined the premises from the outside. Here, give me a hand." I came around the end of the bed and attacked the oddly shaped protuberance. When I saw it through Bell's eyes, I could see it was not symmetrical with the other side of the window. In fact, it proved to be a hidden cupboard. It slid open easily once a purchase on the edge had been managed. In the dark interior we saw that it contained various pieces of clothing, most of it worn and in tatters. "He uses these for going about in disguise, I'll warrant you," he said. Then he saw something which froze him solid for several seconds. He was closer to the open cupboard than I was and could see inside more readily. "I must amend that, Doyle. Here Webb *kept* clothing that he *used* to wear as disguises. My tense was inaccurate. In fact, the past tense is now the appropriate tense for Inspector Webb in the future. Webb has no future. He has lived, as the classical writers say." I moved my head closer to the opening and drew my breath at what I saw. Bell had discovered more than either of us expected. Bell found Webb himself. He had lived, as Bell said. He had become his corpse.

NINETEEN

Once again we were seated in what was becoming our usual places in front of the fireplace in Dr Bell's rooms. Bell was cleaning a cherrywood briar and I was nodding over the recent memory of the steak and kidney pie and the plate of mutton, with which Mrs Murchie had provided us. Perhaps I had taken a drop too much of the excellent port my host provided: Colborne, '64, I think he said.

It was the evening of our discovery of Webb's body. A search of his pockets had revealed nothing more than we had discovered elsewhere in his flat. The man had been strangled with a leather thong ligature which was still embedded deeply in the flesh around the victim's throat. From my limited medical experience, I had suggested that he had been dead less than two hours. The colour and warmth of the body had changed little. Bell had thought that life had been extinguished even more recently. I had deferred to his experience in these matters. He had moved the mandible back and forth, giving the face an almost comic appearance, and had drawn my attention to the facts that neither rigor nor lividity were yet present in the slightest degree. A lifelike shine was still visible on those staring eyes. He had also mentioned the girl we had passed on the stairs, who had indicated that Webb was at home and making noise an hour before our visit.

We had left the rooms as we had entered them. Webb was once more closed within his private locker. He would be found eventually, even in that smelly sty, but the interval gave us an advantage which we discussed over our supper.

"I am not at all comfortable about the fashion in which we left Webb's flat, Joe," I said, seeing the body again in a flash of memory as I set a bone down on the edge of my plate.

"Nor I, Conan. But they must dance barefoot that have no shoes. He said he wanted a wee word in my ear, but that may have been police jiggery-pokery. Remember he was waiting for us with four constables at the tearoom. Others will follow quick enough. This stratagem has bought us a few useful hours. Meanwhile yon Inspector Webb feels no discourtesy. Steel yourself, Conan. We must be practical," he said, then cocking his head to one side asked, "Does your left knee still hurt you so much after all this time? I saw that you favoured the leg as you came to the table."

"It's nothing. I kneeled on something hard in the flat. An occasional twinge, no more."

"Of course!" Bell set his fork and knife down on his plate. "It was the umbrella!"

"Yes, but what of it?"

"It only delivers Webb's murderer to us."

"What?"

"Aye. It was the veiled widow we saw from The Last Minst. She went in with an umbrella and came out without it."

"Inspector Webb was murdered by that woman? I don't believe it."

"That woman wasn't a woman, Conan. It was a disguise. Remember how tall she was? How she used the umbrella as though it were a stick."

This ended the conversation at the table. We spoke no more until we were arranged around the fire and Bell was scratching away at the interior of his briar with a penknife.

"You know, Doyle, I suspect that Lambert senior knows more than the father of the condemned man usually knows. Do you agree?"

"I think what we found in Webb's flat confirms it. He was undoubtedly the source of information about us."

"When a man of dangerously conventional behaviour has had a warning not to interfere, he may panic. He certainly becomes a focus of worry for the villain who requires his obedience. Webb became a similar worry and we saw how he was served. The pressure Lambert brought to bear on the two of us, through the charming intermediary of his daughter, reveals a force exerted on him from some source intended to stiffen even his fused backbone."

"Should we talk to the man? I'm sure he wants to save his son from the gallows."

"Undoubtedly. But, I fear, he would never reveal the source of the pressure. Nor would it amount to more than hearsay when all is done."

"It would indicate a target for our search," I prompted.

"Yes, and warn the villains that we are getting close. No, if we are to pursue the elder Mr Lambert, it must be by indirection. And I think I see a way. Will you be kind enough to hand me the folio of notepaper on the desk beside you."

From this large bundle of notepapers of various shapes and sizes, Bell selected a small half-sheet with the city's crest at the top. On this, with a hasty hand he scribbled the following after only a moment of thought:

> Bell's meddling is becoming serious. Must see you here this evening at 6.30. Dare say no more.
>
> Yrs,

In place of a signature, Bell had made a scrawl which might be taken for any of the letters of the alphabet. He tucked the note into an envelope and affixed a stamp. With a quick reference to the city directory for the address, he was done. "On your way home, drop this into the pillar box closest to the Parliament House. I mention this because I am half afraid you might want to deliver it by hand on the chance of meeting the bonnie Miss Lambert again." I remonstrated with him briefly and we both laughed.

"Lambert, *père*, will get it in the morning and we will be waiting in a cab in front of his house shortly after six o'clock."

"I will not sleep until then," I said.

"Well, laddie, you might spend the midnight hours on your histology with profit. The microscope will tire you if the mere prospect of so much work at this hour does not."

I saw Bell again the following morning in the lecture hall, where I was able to give a fair account of myself in the histology question period, and then, later still, after tea, down the street from the Lambert house. On his instructions, I arrived in good time at the corner of Waterloo Place and Leith Street. A hansom was waiting at the curbstone. Bell was inside, his eyes bright with anticipation of the chase to come. I was glad for the company and for the steep ride up Calton Hill. Bundled up against the cold, we sat in the cab which soon had an excellent view of Lambert's front door. I couldn't help thinking that less than twenty-four hours ago, we had been seated in a low drinking establishment watching another door. I shuddered at the memory of our macabre discovery—that face, the dark, wavy hair and staring eyes, the body propped up inside the cupboard, where, for all I knew, it yet remained.

Lambert's house was an impressive pile, standing out somewhat from its neighbours because of the profusion of ivy climbing its walls. I remarked upon this and was corrected. The vine, it seems, was a species of Virginia creeper introduced into Scotland from America. How he could tell in the dark is only another of the mysteries surrounding my friend.

The night was cool, even in the relative shelter of the interior of a cab. Both of us had thrown a rug over our ulsters which were buttoned to the chin. We kept our eyes trained on anything that moved or appeared to move in Lambert's street. We had been at our post less than ten minutes when the figure of a man came quickly out the front door and headed from Calton Hill towards Canonmill. He was covered by a dark full-length coat, with polished boots showing under it as he walked, and wore an old-fashioned beaver hat on his head at a serious angle. A muffler of grey wool kept his features hidden. Bell ordered the cabbie to keep the man in sight but not to step on his receding heels. Lambert kept up a quick, steady pace. For a man of his years—one could see the grey of his side-whiskers under the gaslight—he set a rugged pace. Without ever turning around, he began to tread the streets leading up the hill. Only once did he stop, to glance at a scrap of paper he produced from a pocket. The area was familiar to him, but I would suggest that he was unsure about the exact house. The cab stopped as he picked his way along Howard Place. Here he turned into the walk leading to number eight, a dark Georgian mansion with a view over the New Town.

"This is no common villain's shiel," I said, breaking a silence of nearly fifteen minutes. Bell ignored the remark and turned the pages of the city directory which he had brought with him. He handed me the bull's-eye lantern, then closed the book with a low whistle.

"What is it?" I asked.

"My suspicions are confirmed," he whispered. "Confirmed in general. But even I did not imagine that the trail would lead us here."

"I can see power and position written on the walls and windows, but what else do you see, Doctor?"

"This is the wee abode of Sir William Burnham, QC, KCB, the Procurator-Fiscal of the Shire of Midlothian!"

"It can't be!" I gasped. "He, if anyone, is above suspicion."

"No man, nor woman neither, is above suspicion, laddie. But this would account for the well-managed campaign being waged against us: my little talk with the principal of the university and your tumble in the back street near the Cowgate, not to mention the man standing in the shadows at the back of the museum across from my house."

On the way back to Bell's rooms in Lothian Street, I contemplated our enemy: Sir William Burnham. What did I know of him? Very little, and yet, at the same time, I do not recall a time when his name was unknown to me. I remembered the pink face from the first day of Lambert's trial. Sir William was a part of the landscape, like the Castle as seen from the Grassmarket, and almost as durable. His name was often in the papers, usually in connection with an important civic event. His comings and goings were marked in the column usually devoted to the court circular. He was the keystone of that outwardly respectable and inwardly corrupt world that Stevenson spoke about. He had called the city a sty, a cesspool, with all of its officials vampires. I was forced to imagine Sir William Burnham with one or another of his arms reaching into the herring barrel of corruption.

I had seen Burnham's magnificent estate in Fifeshire. It had been pointed out to me on a summer ramble with my family several years ago. We heard shooting on the large grouse moor and caught sight of several of the beaters as they made their way home at the end of the day.

While I was thus musing, Bell beside me was fidgeting. I asked him what was toward. He replied with a smile. "Does that spy in the bushes across the street from me still disquiet you?" he asked. I admitted that he did waylay my thoughts more than I liked.

"I think I know how to dislodge this unwelcome limpet, Doyle. Lend me your hat."

"My hat? What are you—?" Bell placed a finger on my lips and gave a reassuring twist to his head. All the while he was readjusting his clothing and brushing his usually tidy hair until it was plastered over his balding head. He fixed it there with saliva. Under my hat, it appeared as a fringe, which quite altered his appearance. He tore his pocket handkerchief into several pieces and inserted one balled fragment into each of his cheeks. I marvelled as he tried out several distorted expressions in his pocket mirror, each one an invented emotion to suit some imagined situation.

"Is this a rehearsal for some amateur theatricals, Doctor?"

"I resent the word 'amateur' in the context, Doyle. I pride myself on my ability to alter my appearance. I have often done it for the academic procession at June convocation. No one seemed to notice. Of course, I had no idea that it would ever prove to be of more practical use."

"This must have something to do with that fellow outside your house," I said.

"Capital! You too are catching on to this singular game. How is it possible that I never tried it before?"

"You mean, if Graeme Lambert had not come to see you, this side of your personality would have remained forever buried?"

"Forever is a muckle wee bit of time, Doyle. I should not like to judge of that. And I was forgetting the singular business of the Dean's telescope, which I must tell you about one day."

The cab had now crossed the George IV Bridge. Bell

banged upon the roof for the driver to stop and we got out
into the dismal, nearly empty street. Bell paid the driver
from his coin purse and we tasted our heels for some
distance, sending out smoky blasts of warm air into the
cold night air. When we were in sight of his house, Bell
urged me into a dark doorway in the façade of the museum. With a finger laid to one side of his nose and a whispered "Shush!" he was off down the street by himself. He
had altered his accustomed pace and, I know that this will
sound absurd, even his height had been altered: for he
walked with a strut that resembled that of a military man
in his retirement, a soldier on half-pay. Breathless, I
watched him go directly to a dark shadow across from the
light coming from Bell's windows. A dark figure stepped
out of the shadows for a moment and then both figures
were swallowed up into the blackness of the night.

With the light coming from Bell's rooms adding distorted oblongs of light on the pavement, I lifted my eyes to
those windows, for something about one of them caught a
portion of my attention, but had failed for a moment to
convey to my brain the significance of what was to be seen
there. I looked more attentively and nearly cried out. For
there, for all to see, sat Dr Joseph Bell! His shadow could
easily be seen against the drawn blind. I looked away to the
spot where my friend had been a moment before, but could
make out nothing. The darkness was as unbroken as
before. In the first-floor window, my friend seemed to be
nodding over the book he was examining. I was about to
ignore my instructions and cross to his front door, when I
saw a figure emerge from the shadows. It was the spy. I flat-
tened my back against the door of my alcove hiding-place.
The spy passed within three feet of me and continued down
the street and out of sight. Moments later, Bell himself
appeared, beckoning me to follow. He crossed to his door

and waited. My progress was prolonged by my inability to keep my eyes off the silhouette of my friend already seated in his own bay-window and at the same time searching for his latchkey in his pocket in the street below.

TWENTY

The mystery was quickly solved when we were again seated in Bell's rooms. Mounted on a pedestal table, whose height had been increased by several thick medical tomes, sat a Fowler's Phrenology head with a few paper additions held in place with sticking plaster. "Come in and meet Dr Joseph Bell, Doyle. He does rather well, doesn't he? I altered the shape of the nose and chin as well as giving a suggestion of hair. Otherwise, a Fowler head does very well."

I examined the head more carefully. It was the familiar object with its map of the cerebral cortex marked off with boundaries like a political map of the cantons of Switzerland. To this, cut-outs which more closely represented Bell's face had been applied, as I have already said. A lamp had been placed directly behind the figure so that a sharp outline, similar to the silhouettes we used to make of children on a rainy afternoon, was cast upon the blind.

"Ingenious, but simple," Bell said, moving the figure slightly on its perch, so as to present a slightly different effect.

"So much for the mystery of your being in two places at once, Doctor. Now tell me what you said to the spy to get him to leave his post."

"Oh, that? I simply took him aside and put a bug in his ear."

"It must have been a giant beetle to get him to leave without authorization."

"A cerambycid called the aberrant long-horned beetle would be about the correct size for the commission I gave him."

"Commission?"

"Doyle, my good fellow, do you hear an echo in here, or am I going slowly deaf?" I must have blushed, because suddenly my collar seemed a size too small. But, Bell's joke was easily swallowed when he rang for his housekeeper, who brought up the first of a succession of trays, which she placed on the table Bell and I hastily cleared of books and papers.

During the soup, perhaps to put me off the scent of our enquiry, Bell told me that he had heard from the runaway George Budd in Plymouth in the morning post: he had married the wench I had seen and was setting up his medical practice there on the south coast.

"He's a brilliant sort of eccentric," said my friend, "but I must say I'm not unhappy he's gone. I've never met a more insensitive human being. He is like a boot demanding an apology from the toes it recently trampled. He will make a spectacular success of medicine, I suspect, but it won't be because of his skill in the profession. He has too little patience to win many patients. He'll find the necessary megaphone to shout his quack cures. But, there's more than that. I believe he has started experimenting with cocaine. I have seen it in his eyes. He has never shown more than the customary malevolence to me, his teacher. Still, I don't quite trust the fellow. Never did. There's a mean, vindictive stripe down his back. And you know how arrogant he can be."

"Poor girl," I said.

"*Mrs* George Turnavine Budd, my friend. A Ward in Chancery no longer, unless they are discovered."

During the fish course, Bell dissected the head of his fish while giving an impromptu lecture on asymmetry. "In the flat-fishes, as Huxley so ably points out, the skull becomes so completely distorted that the two eyes lie on one side of the body. Take your plaice, now. Pleuronectidae. In certain of these fishes, Doyle, the rest of the skull and facial bones—please examine the bones under my fork—yes, and even the spine and limbs partake of the same asymmetry. How do you find it? Is it to your taste?"

"I'm afraid that mine is getting cold."

"Well, eat up! Eat up, laddie! I'll no' have you letting a nice bit of plaice go to waste. But tell me about your wanting to become a doctor. Is this the wish of your childhood being realized?" Over the rest of the fish and then on into the roasted woodcock with boiled potatoes and greens, I told him about my ambitions. I made him privy to the small successes that I had had with some articles and stories. We were finishing a hot apple tart when Bell wiped his chin and spoke again.

"So, you don't see yourself lancing carbuncles for the next fifty years when you could be writing stories. What sorts of stories, laddie?"

"I've always been fired up by tales of chivalry. And of the Napoleonic Wars. The Monmouth Rebellion. What I wouldn't give to have been there!"

"There's always a new war coming up the drafty turnpike, Doyle. Dinna wish too hard. You narrowly missed the Crimea and China. Perhaps you'd like to join General Gordon in suppressing the slave trade in the Sudan, Abyssinia and central Africa. These are brave times for the Empire, Doyle. Take care your eyes are not closed. While France is crippled and the Germans stand beguiled by their victory, while America is recovering from its family dispute, now is the time for Russia to snatch at the east. And everywhere our empire is in its way. Disraeli sees that. That's why he is trying to woo Ismail Pasha to part with the Suez Canal. There're real stories enough for you brewing in the next few years."

"I want to write about the Forty-five. It's our own

history and who is to write it now Scott's in his tomb?"

"And he has that monument, like a Chinese rocket, on Princes Street. You have a friend, young Stevenson; he's anither like you! Canna be two like that, God knows. Has he been blowing in your ear?"

"We both want to get on, Doctor. And we see that we would like to do it with our pens. Perhaps the lancet will help support my muse. I don't know how it will work itself out, sir. But I am bound to complete what I have started here."

"Good! Do you think you would like to try a cigar?"

"Gladly. But I hope you don't imagine that I have forgotten about the spy across the street. I want to know what you told him to send him on his way."

"Och, that. It's a thing of no special significance. I told him that he should warn the deputy chief constable that Scotland Yard is showing an interest in this case and might be sending someone to Edinburgh to investigate."

"Wonderful! Is it true?"

"Of course not, Doyle. But he doesn't know that."

TWENTY-ONE

I was looking up everything I could find about Sir William Burnham in the free library. It was a fine old family to be sure. Not Scottish, but there were many of the "Auld Enemy" around about who had taken a bite of the haggis and not gagged. One Burnham invented a high-pressure air lock, another was a hero at Balaclava. A third was a Baptist preacher, who threw himself against the rock of the Presbytery often enough to finally retire impotent and wasted to Bournemouth at the age of thirty-five. A Burnham had been allied with Montrose, another assisted in the Highland clearances. Another group of Burnhams had distinguished themselves in local government: a Staffordshire sheriff, a bailiff from Worcestershire and so on. They appeared on councils from the ranks of solicitors and advocates. In the last century, for a time, one of that name, as Lord Provost, may be said to have "ruled" Edinburgh. Of course it didn't last. Nothing does. But there were other Burnhams back again in high places not twenty years later. As Procurator-Fiscal, Sir William was enormously powerful.

My recollection of his Fifeshire estate, interrupted by Bell in the cab, as he slipped into his contrived disguise, became for me the symbol of the man I had seen at the opening day of Lambert's trial. But, suddenly, the absurdity of my work was brought home to me. How ridiculous, how silly of me to be wasting not only my own time, but the much more valuable time of Alan Lambert, in this improbable pursuit. In science we learn to reject absurd propositions. Unequal things may not be compared successfully. Why should a powerful man persecute this blameless young man into his grave? With what object? They lived in different spheres. What possible connection could Burnham have with Mlle Clery, apart from his box overlooking the stage at the opera house. Perhaps they had met at a reception. She was most attractive and the toast of the city. Could some irregular relationship have existed? Edinburgh was famous for being a town where the right hand quickly forgot what the left was doing. Could such gossip be suppressed?

Clearly, more work needed to be done here. My tower of speculative filigree required buttressing before it began to shake and fall. It needed hard facts or, failing that, hearsay of a respectable sort. What did I know of a certainty? The affections of Mlle Clery had been conferred upon another: the poor fellow who shared her fate. Would it be likely that the Procurator-Fiscal would share a mistress with a minor clerk in some drab department of public works? I tried to imagine my poor father, in days of more robust health, competing with some great civic official for the favours of a Mlle Clery. I could not see it.

When a public official stoops to folly...Scottish history is rich in examples. History is in general. I must not be too quick to call absurd what merely looks absurd.

Louise Lambert was seated in my place in the library when I arrived with my satchel of papers and books. She looked at me with wide eyes. "Any news?" she whispered, taking my hand in hers.

"There's too much to say and so much to be done that I have no time to tell you. Have you eaten your dinner?"

"I'm engaged," she pouted, and added, when she saw my expression, "A dear aunt from Aberdeen." That made me feel better. Then I had an idea.

"Louise, remember you told me about an amateur play

you saw a few nights ago. Could you repeat what you said?
There was something in your description that caught my
mind."

"But not your memory it seems."

"Be a dear and tell me again."

"I thought it was well done. Some of Graeme's old
friends were in it. People you don't know, like David
M'Clung and Henry Burgoyne. Is that what you want to
hear?"

"Yes, tell me the rest."

"That's about all. Graeme hated it, but Graeme won't
admit that Andrew Burnham is a fine amateur actor.
They've hated one another since they were children.
Andrew is really very good. You should have seen him at
the Scobbie masquerade, he was quite ravishing, although,
of course, father thought he went too far."

"Why was that?"

"He was too good. Father said it made him feel peculiar. I just wanted to know who had done his hair."

Instead of having a bite to eat, when Louise left to meet
her aunt, I wandered over to the Opera House and then
around the corner to the nearest tavern, The Wounded
Stag, where I found stagehands with a dark pint in almost
every hand standing at the bar and chattering choristers
tuning their pipes with sherry. I was looking for Jasper Ballantyne, who had failed his second year medicine and then,
in a fit of melancholy, attached himself to the theatre as a
man of all work. As long as his strong back supported him,
he would be employed.

Ballantyne was standing at the far end of the bar, holding an empty glass in his hand. I approached, clapped him
on the back, and ordered two pints from the barman, who
looked as though he would rather be in some other
business. His disapproval of his customers—perhaps it was

of drinking itself!—was evident in every line in his face. Jasper Ballantyne, on the other hand, enjoyed his vices. Unfortunately, his face was beginning to show it. There were now bluish deeps to his eye sockets, and the colour in his cheeks had faded. When I remarked on the latter in a joking way, he protested that the theatre was indoor work and that I should not be surprised by theatrical pallor. He offered the pale faces of his companions as proofs of his assertion. The choristers, already made up for the matinée, we agreed to disqualify from the argument, although with our backs to the bar the lot of them made far more attractive viewing than our own features reflected in the mirror behind the bar.

After some pleasantries and reminiscences of our days in medical school, I got quickly to the point of my visit. "Was Mlle Clery involved with anyone apart from poor Gordon Eward? Did she have an older and richer patron?"

"I didn't know her well, Artie, although I would have liked to: she was a bonnie bit, y'know." I gritted my teeth together when I heard him call me by that puerile diminutive, but kept listening. "Hew M'Chesney, over there, would be better to talk to. They say he cried at the news of her murder." Jasper made the necessary introductions and I repeated my questions to a big man with a face as large and as red as a kerchief and with wee, pale blue eyes that did not quite belong.

"She wass a lady first and always an artist in efferything," he said. "In France and other places, she had a string of stage-door-Johnnys, some of them fery well fixed, you know: toffs from Charlotte Square, viscounts and the Honourable this and the Honourable that. She lived with a writer once, a poet, in the rue Scribe in Paris, but that was to get him to finish the opera he promised to write for her. But when she met wee Gordie, down in Menton, efferything changed. You see, Gordie knew his music. She said that Gordie had the face a Gounod should write for. No, sir, after she met Gordie, there were no more successful followers and no more stage-door-Johnnys."

"And Hew would know if she did. There are no well-kept secrets in an opera company," assured my old university friend. I nodded my thanks and began to turn away; the beer having robbed me of half my list of questions.

"Hew, you dinna mention Cabezon."

"What's he to the purpose?"

"Let Artie decide. Mario Cabezon is a singing teacher. He gives lessons in Dewar Place. Mlle Clery studied with him in Milan." I made note of the name to be polite, but I couldn't see our chase moving in that direction at this late date.

"When would that have been?" I asked.

"From before she first appeared in Milan."

"They say he was like a sculptor modelling the way she sang, the way she walked and talked."

"He wass more Mephisto than Cellini. It wass Faust with a soprano singing the leading part."

"It was all over by the time she came here, of course. One of the shortest marriages on record."

"Marriage! He *married* Hermione Clery? When was that?"

"Seven years ago. And they are still legally man and wife. There are no divorces under the papist steeples of Italy."

"So Mlle Clery is, or was, legally Signora Mario Cabezon? And you say he lives here in Edinburgh?"

"Cabezon was a Pygmalion jealous of every note his Galatea sang. After their separation, he followed her efferywhere: Rome, Paris, New York and finally here to Edinburgh at the beginning off the season. He had a box effery night she sang."

"Was Cabezon here on the night she was murdered?"

"Odd the police neffer brought him into it. I wondered about that, I did."

"What's all this about, Artie?" said my friend, with a hand on my lapel. "Old Marwood's coming to town on Thursday. He's going to swing young Lambert on the new drop. Never been used before. Lambert will baptize it for all who'll come after."

"Marwood, the man from Horncastle," said Hew, to no one in particular. "Time wass we had a proper Scots hangman. Didn't need to share with the Sassenach. Now we can't stretch a neck without a by-your-leave from Whitehall. But what do you expect? It's just a mite of Scottish taxes that are spent in Scotland." I did not try to stem this line of talk. I knew it had to play itself out.

In a moment one of the choristers, a dark-eyed beauty with her hair pinned up, a pinched waist, and wearing a *pince-nez* with the black ribbon pinned to her blouse, joined us. She had heard the talk about the execution, and wished to add her own bit of lore. "You ken what they say about a hanged man, don't you, Jasper?" she said with a meaningful smile as she stood closer to the man than necessary.

"What is there to know about?" he asked. "He won't be buying a round of drinks after Marwood does his job. Would you like to see it, Mrs Gibson?" I was formally introduced to the woman, Flora Gibson, chorister and understudy to the supporting lead soprano. She managed to look rather prim under her theatrical make-up and rather exciting at the same time.

"I don't see why they hide it away from the public, Jasper. They could do anything to the poor man and we never the wiser. At least, he'll have one last jolt of joy, just as the lights go out."

"Are you daft, woman? What are you on about?"

"Oh, then I see that the great Mr Ballantyne has not completed his education. If you're nice to me and buy me a sherry, just a little one, I might be persuaded to tell you." The young woman looked at me as though she thought I might come between her and the glass of sherry she was soon holding. The talk spun away from me and I let it ramble without noticing more than the expression on the faces of those around me. When the conversation flagged a few minutes later, I remembered another of my questions.

"What do you know about Eward, apart from his pretty face and knowledge of music?" Hew considered this for a moment.

"Nothing at all. He wassn't one of us, wass he? He kept accounts in the City Chambers. A copybook-blotter, that's what he wass. Could add and subtract and efferything, I reckon. A harmless idiot, a *bampot*, that's what he wass from what I hear." Flora Gibson followed our talk with her eyes, as though it were a tennis match.

"And where was it you heard that?" I asked. Hew wiped foam from his mouth by applying his sleeve to the affected area and drawing it along until the buttons stung his lips. Mrs Gibson shot me a conspiratorial smile, but clung to Jasper. She tried to change the subject:

"I saw a couple topped together when I was a girl in Glasgow," she said, returning to a more piquant line of conversation. She was leaning with her back against the rim of the bar so that the pattern of her camisole could be seen etched beneath the fabric of her blouse. "It didn't frighten me a bit. The preacher had just married them as they stood together on the drop. Her name was Blackwood. I forget his name, but, then, she didn't have it long, did she? She shouted 'I will!' and the hangman dropped her and her new husband through the floor!" Jasper and Hew stared at the woman, who was nearing the bottom of her ladylike glass of sherry. "He was dead in a few minutes, but it took her longer. Ever thought what it would be like, Hew?"

He returned Flora Gibson a wry smile, then looked at me. "You want to speak to John James M'Dougal in the Board of Works about Eward. He kens a thing or two, that one. Tell him I sent you."

I made my departure at the next convenient moment and returned to the library after finding a shop in a close down a lane that would make me a sandwich. I was tempted to follow the lead Hew had given me, and wanted to inform Bell of the discovery of Sr Cabezon, but I found young Biggar waiting for me when I got back to my place.

"Himself has a message for you," he said, looking put out and aggrieved, which I must say became Biggar.

"You mean Dr Bell?" I asked.

"Who else would be having me traipse all over town looking for you in all your secret holes? He said that it is extremely important and that you would know what it was about. He didn't tell me."

"Thank you, John. I know how Dr Bell relies on you and trusts you in these matters," I said, trying unsuccessfully to mollify his jealousy. "What is the message?"

"You are to meet him at Waverley Station at 4:00 to catch the 4:15 train for York. Pack a bag and don't be late." I thanked Biggar and packed up my notes. I returned home and asked Bridget to put some clothes into a club bag for me. I was unsure whether this was to be a one-day excursion or one lasting two or more. Lambert's appointment with the hangman made me certain that it was not for the rest of the week.

Given the lateness of the hour, I hailed a cab and told

him to hurry to the station. The day had already lost its light and lamps were being lit in the shops along the streets we drove through. The yellow reek of the town stood like a coloured gauze between me and the illuminated gas lamps, which looked out of focus and indistinct because of the mist. The fog gives us a new refraction, making seeing difficult, like trying to see through a snowstorm.

Bell was in the station with his housekeeper who was giving him instructions and impressing upon him, or trying to, the contents of his bag and the whereabouts of the tickets she placed in one of his inside pockets. He nodded and gesticulated and told her that he understood all of these things and would miss the train if she was determined to go over them again for the fourth time. "Ah, Doyle! I'm glad you got the message. I have the tickets. Don't look so surprised. I will explain everything when we are aboard. Thank you, Mrs Murchie. You have been most kind!"

"I've put your pills in your bag and an extra pouch of tobacco under your pyjamas."

"Mrs Murchie, really! I must protest. You are too kind." Bell slipped me a wink and together we bade her goodbye and headed in the direction of the ticket controllers at the gate leading to the lines. Inside the station, the light was of the submarine sort that made one hurry to get through it. A large illuminated clock told the hour as men and women came along the platforms towards or from the coaches. Satanic engines spat out clouds of white vapour, as though trying to show the rest of the city the way proper fog ought to look. A little man walked along banging the wheels with a hammer, waiting for the dull sound of a cracked or broken one.

With Bell's hand on my sleeve, we found the right track and a compartment in a coach of the right train. We were five minutes before the departure time, but by the time the train began to move, like a dead monster suddenly reanimated, we had placed our belongings on the racks above our heads, adjusted our bodies and settled into the mode most convenient for travel.

"Why, Dr Bell, are we hurtling out into the dark bound towards York this night?" I asked.

"A perfectly natural question. Also an obvious one. You'll remember me speaking of the need to bring in a specialist at the time I wrote to my old student, Monty Corry? Well, Monty is the private secretary of the prime minister. The truth is, and I cannot say I am not excited by the prospect, that we are going to a rendezvous with the prime minister."

"The prime minister? Do you mean we are meeting with Disraeli?"

"Lord Beaconsfield he is now. Much the same. Here, read over Monty's telegram while I consult my Bradshaw's in another matter." Here he pulled the familiar yellow-wrapped volume from his bag and riffled through its pages, all the while continuing to address me: "Dizzy is the specialist I told you about. Do you remember?" I held the telegram in front of my eyes, but I could see no writing. The thought that I was on my way to see Benjamin Disraeli destroyed in me all thought, all desire. All I could do was babble and stare ahead.

TWENTY-TWO

As soon as the train came to a complete stop in York's station, a conductor quickly showed us the way through gasps of steam from an engine to the stationmaster, who was watching for us as the train emptied about a third of its passengers and began to take on more than that many again for the rest of the journey south.

During the journey, I had had ample opportunity to describe in detail to my friend all that had passed since our last meeting. The revelations of The Wounded Stag were of particular interest and they opened up avenues of enquiry that we could follow as soon as the current adventure was concluded. Bell was amused by my description of Mrs Flora Gibson. "This must be regarded, Doyle, as a primitive mating ritual, or an approach to one. Your friend had better be on his guard. The woman seems dedicated to arousing his amorous propensities, as Dr Johnson once said about the same sort of theatrical persons. Helen Blackwood was executed twenty-six years ago. I doubt that Mrs Gibson was giving a very reliable account of the event, unless, of course, in your delightful description of the woman, you subtracted several years from her age." I felt shamed and undone. I thought that I had hidden a momentary infatuation with the captivating singer with more skill.

The stationmaster saluted Bell and asked us to follow him, which we did. He led us to the end of the platform on the extreme right end of the station, just under the high wall. The platform continued, uncovered a few hundred yards beyond this point and ended where a train of perhaps three or four cars was awaiting us. A bobby with a rosy face was already in place at the end of the last car. We were helped aboard by the stationmaster and a tall lean man of thirty-five or forty, who had appeared from the coach.

"Joe! Joe Bell! How are you, my dear chap, how are you?" The speaker's smile disarmed me at once, as he enfolded his old friend in both arms. Joe introduced me to Montague Corry, who was a veritable warming-oven of goodwill as he brought us into the carriage, which was arranged as a drawing-room rather than the usual compartments.

He had the lineaments and bearing of an aristocrat, and having understood that, he made no further claim upon either his forebears or his high position. His greeting, in which I shared, couldn't have been more friendly had we been long-lost cousins. Once the railway people had bowed out, he settled us into stuffed chairs and explained what was about to happen. In this there was nothing of the major-domo; one didn't feel handled or processed. He told us, almost as though he were describing the rules of a new and wonderful game, that the prime minister was resting now, but that in about twenty minutes, perhaps less, he would awaken and take some light refreshment. At that time, he would take us to him.

My imagined pictures of the great involved endlessly receding corridors and liveried servants opening up one double door after another until the august presence is glimpsed enthroned at the far end of his *sanctum sanctorum*. Here in this simple railway car, the slightest suggestion of the pomp and circumstance of the Congress of Berlin or of the dignity of the office of prime minister was absent. Here all was business. I saw red despatch boxes and cartons of files labelled with the names of government departments. The difference between the imagined fiction and the flat-footed reality made my head spin.

Corry was already in conversation with Bell. From his questions I could see that he was as well versed in the affair as we were. He knew to the hour how much time remained to Alan Lambert. He explained the procedure by which the Home Office could be notified should we find the proofs necessary to grant a reprieve. He described the sort of evidence that would be required.

"It's not enough, you see, to illuminate various facets of the case that didn't come out at the trial. What you'll need is hard, incontrovertible evidence that the court has rendered a wrong sentence. This must be based on new evidence, germane to the core of the enquiry. For instance, Dr Bell, it would not be enough to show that the culprit's name was wrongly recorded or that he was incorrectly detained prior to having his charges read out to him."

"Monty, when did you know me to be a fiddler with the edges of the picture. I am sure that we will be able to demonstrate that our man is innocent beyond a shadow of a doubt, just as he was found guilty in the face of a blizzard of doubt on almost every point raised in this prosecution."

"The fact that there is no normal channel of appeal for Scottish cases is in your favour. But, when this step is taken, it is fair for me to tell you more convictions are upheld than are overturned. You are not out of danger, Joe. You are not acting without risk."

"He is walking a tightrope without a net, my dear Corry. Good evening, gentlemen. Dr Bell, a real pleasure! Mr, soon-to-be Doctor Doyle. I have and value a portrait your uncle made of me; one of those foolish treasures that makes living worth all the dressing and undressing. No, don't get up. I intend to join you at once. I try to be ever at my ease." It was Disraeli, of course! So informal and yet at once so familiar. Here was the familiar face, with its

darkish parchment skin and bright black eyes, the high
forehead, the little curl in the middle, the stooped and stu-
dious posture. Disraeli, or as I should say, Lord Beaconsfield, for so he had been for the last three years, looked like
a caricature by Leach, Dicky Doyle, Vincent or Ape come
to life from the pages of *Punch* or *Spy*. Dressed in solemn
black, there was nothing solemn about his bearing or
expression. He noted the way I was regarding him, probably noticing that my jaw had dropped from the intensity of
the surprise. "Don't believe it, sir," he said. "You *are* seeing things: I am in fact the ghost of myself, an emanation.
Or, if you prefer, you may set me down as the Canadian
prime minister, whom I much resemble, if that would be
easier on your spirits." He smiled at Corry and at Bell,
whom he leaned over to pat on the knee. "Monty came to
me talking about you fifteen years ago and has continued
this tattoo of unbridled praise without recess ever since. I
call upon you to stem the flow of his adulation. You have
done me a great service in coming here." We all laughed at
this, and it helped to expel the pressure in the carriage as
air suddenly released from a caisson.

"Dr Bell, I don't know whether you are aware of it, but
the first detective in all the world, if you exclude the
prophet Daniel, was a Scot like yourself: I am referring to
Mr Lincoln's indefatigable Mr Pinkerton. His youthful
involvement with the Chartists was the cause of his leaving
Glasgow for the New World."

"I am not, sir, properly speaking, a detective. I have certain skills, a capacity to deduce the unknown from what is
known. That is all."

"Doctor, you will never pull down in ten minutes what
Monty has been all these years building. Besides, there is no
stigma attached to it. The detective is the modern knight
errant. His quest, not a fair maiden in distress—not

necessarily—but justice itself. I will happily drink a toast to the profession. Ah, and I see that now I can."

A servant in a gold-and-black striped waistcoat appeared with a bottle of claret in a silver bucket, and reappeared in a moment with a tray of sandwiches.

"I should rather enjoy being a ghost sometime. Right now I could blow Gladstone's papers off his podium in Midlothian where he is again ranting about my government. Not that he ever sticks to a text any more than he does to a principle or a policy.

"I won't name him, but I have a general, a celebrated officer, most distinguished. I fear that he too would like to be a ghost. Or perhaps it is martyrdom he is seeking. I don't think I could conscientiously ask men to follow such an officer. I refused to play Pontius Pilate to his Jesus Christ. So, I've got him a staff job close to home and intend to leave him there.

"But, I see that time is short, Dr Bell. Please tell me at once how I may help you without turning the constitution of these shires into a sorry stew."

"I've explained what our limited powers are, sir."

"Of course, Monty, of course. I assumed you had. Dr Bell," he continued, "the Home Office is very jealous of its rights and powers and rather slack in its duties. It is, in other words, a typical government department. For over one hundred years Scotland has been maintained by the department that could mount the least good argument for escaping that nasty burden. I say 'nasty' simply because after centuries of neglect, Scotland requires far more attention than any ministry can well afford. I personally love Scotland in spite of her Whiggish universities. The dear Queen adores her. Would that we could settle upon her what her deserts are. But a cabinet is a brougham surrounded by squeaking wheels each noisier than the last.

The pinions of possibility girdle us until we faint with fatigue. In law matters, the Home Secretary is advised by a man in charge of Scottish affairs, and by the Lord Advocate, Sir George Currie, the chief law officer in Edinburgh. Now, in this case, the Lord Advocate himself managed the prosecution. Quite rightly, he should have disqualified himself from giving advice on the matter and advising that commission you helped get started. But there's nothing to be gained when your law lord tastes his ambition as keenly as this one does. He'd order the salmon *and* the plaice at your dinner. In a word, he's not to be trusted. Oh, I dare say he's honest enough, patriotic, doesn't kick his dogs or educate his daughters, but he lacks vision. It's a common enough deficiency. When I first got to my feet to speak in the House, I was shouted down so fast it made my ears ring. But I told them that the day would come when they would listen. And they have been listening."

"Sir," interrupted Monty Corry, "the Scotland train leaves in ten minutes."

"About my brain," said Mr Disraeli with a twinkle. "I haven't given you your say, sir. The floor is yours." Bell replaced the sandwich in his fingers on a sidetable before speaking:

"I wish to impress upon you, sir, the urgency of what happens upon our return. Only a few hours remain. And we have discovered that we are dealing with desperate men. Already a policeman, who had failed to deter us, has been murdered. They will stop at nothing." Here Bell leaned forward and spoke to the prime minister in a voice so low that I couldn't hear what he was saying. Disraeli nodded and listened. Once he caught Bell by the lapels and insisted on adding a word of his own. Now it was Bell's turn to nod and listen. At last, they settled back in their chairs and resumed speaking normally. The prime minister began:

"You are dealing with people, Dr Bell, who think that the way to save the nation is to pretend that the nation never makes mistakes. Far better to crush an innocent idiot who gets stuck in the works than shout out 'Stop the machine!' They imagine, in their ignorance, that the world will think better of us if we have a home park full of buried atrocities than if we admit that we are still trying to get this peculiar cultivator called government to work without breaking down. As though governments aren't always breaking down. Take mine, for instance. But you haven't time to hear that. No! Put me back on the road, Monty! Where was I?"

"Tell Dr Bell what you are prepared to do, sir."

"Good! I would like to say, sir, that I will pluck your young client out of jail and set his feet on the street again. I cannot. The Home Secretary acts independently in these matters. The cabinet doesn't come into it. There is no open discussion. I cannot take him aside and whisper in his ear. Not *this* Home Secretary! But I am a past master of the arts of indirection. You may count upon it that I will, by means best known to myself, alert the Home Office to the fact that new evidence is about to appear and that the mechanism to stop the execution can instantly be put into motion as soon as the Home Office is notified. To that end I have placed the senior Queen's messenger at your disposal. In fact, Monty tells me, he will be journeying north on the same train as William Marwood, the executioner. Curious, isn't it? I wonder if they will meet and talk?"

While Mr Dizzy, as he was affectionately called in my home, had been talking, the tray of sandwiches was passed from one lap to the next. Wine was poured from a bottle marked "Lafitte." There was no small talk. Corry glanced only twice at his watch. Suddenly, Lord Beaconsfield was on his feet and shaking both of us warmly by the hand,

and, without the feeling of being hurried, we left the rail-way car and the siding. Glancing back, we could see Dis-raeli standing there in the doorway of the carriage, as though he were making us the present of a memory. It was an inspired piece of *mise en scène*, but completely without side. No egotism was on display; it was a simple gift. We turned and waved our hats. He returned the wave with the napkin he took from his chin, perhaps sending Downing Street crumbs onto the ways.

TWENTY-THREE

We had cleared the station and the dark silhouette of the city of York fell behind us before Bell spoke. Since we found a compartment and made ourselves reasonably comfortable, my friend had been buried in deep thought. He had brought his long fingers together, tip to tip, and settled his head well back on the cushion with his eyes shut tight.

For my part, I tried to run the minutes in the private train back again in my mind, the way I tried to imagine my boxing bouts, blow by blow, from some neutral position. It improved my form in the ring, certainly, but I became aware that my form was only part of the equation. I was rarely as strong as the other fellow, so my blows counted for less. Nor was I quick to see what my opponent was dishing out for me in time to do anything about it. In this way, I reweighed every phrase and expression that passed on that masklike visage, attempting, perhaps, to see at second hand what I had missed the first time.

"He's not a well man."

"What?" Bell's sudden utterance guillotined my reverie.

"Lord Beaconsfield. He's ailing."

"But—!" I protested.

"I know, I know. He hides it well. And the spirit shines through. Nevertheless…"

"Is there any danger?"

"He appears to be in the grip of a homoeopath who has done him some good, but this arsenic-eating—even a mild course—gives him the appearance of health without the reality."

"You could tell all that in a few minutes?"

"Oh, yes. It's all there to be seen: the asthma and bronchitis, the insomnia and, I'm afraid, Richard Bright's Disease."

"But you can't be certain?"

"Doyle, you know my methods. Do you wish to hear the details?"

"More to the point, how was Lord Beaconsfield able to help us?"

"Ah! That was a rare glimpse of a consummate politician."

"Are you saying that he gave the appearance of help without the substance?"

"Doyle, my friend! So young and so cynical! I can hardly credit it!" Here he roared with laughter while my collar felt distinctly uncomfortable. I had not meant to be clever; the words fell from me without thought.

In under five hours, we were back in Edinburgh's yellow fog and the reek of a hundred thousand chimneys. It was cold, made colder by a bitter wind blowing from the north-east. We shared a cab as far as Lothian Street, where Bell left me, and I continued with the cab home.

"There's been police here lookin' for you, Mr Arthur," said Bridget when I came in at the door.

"There was two of 'em last night and two again this morning, sir." I concluded that Webb's body had been uncovered. Bell knew when we put the body back in its cupboard that the time the postponed discovery gave us was but slight. A day or two at the most. Perhaps Webb's efforts against Joe Bell and me were being taken up by other hands. Whichever case applied, I decided that a good hot bath separated me from all rational thought and sensible precautions. I gave Bridget instructions accordingly and she curtsied, as she often did when we were alone in the house together, and ran to draw my bath.

An hour later, I was walking down Lothian Street, newly bathed and wearing fresh clothing. The grit of the railway journey had been left behind, but the source of fresh perspiration was contained in the newspaper I carried. Here the discovery of Webb's body was confirmed. Neighbours had been alerted to the open door and the odour coming from Webb's flat. Our descriptions were given in some detail, but our names were not mentioned. It would have been foolish to imagine that the police were ignorant of our identities. As I was hurrying down Lothian Street, I knew the grave importance of telling Dr Bell of the policemen who were looking for me. Undoubtedly, they would be looking for him as well. As though to prove what I had said, I rounded a corner and saw two police inspectors—they couldn't be anything else in those uniformlike "plain clothes"—coming from Bell's house. Mrs Murchie was seeing them off the premises. In doing so, she spied me as I stood still in my tracks, as though struck by lightning. The policemen re-entered their four-wheeler and drove off, and Bell's front door opened again, with the good Mrs Murchie waving me across the street. After examining the prospect on both sides to see whether there were other eyes on Bell's front door, I crossed to the house. Mrs Murchie reached into her ample bosom and produced a note written in Bell's hand:

> We are hard-pressed and no time is to be lost. Meet me in front of the City Chambers as soon as you can. I will be in the small second-hand bookshop across the way. Be careful not to lead the authorities in this direction. All is lost if we are detained by the police.
>
> Bell

I should have taken a cab, but not seeing one immediately to hand, I began hurrying on foot towards the City Chambers. My intention was to hail transport when I saw some for hire, but I did not spy anything of the kind until I was well across George IV Bridge near The Lawnmarket, by which time a cab would have been redundant. The few hundred yards down the High Street to my objective I took at a good clip. In the frosty air, I could see my breath in great round puffs of vapour, rather more like the exhalation of a racing horse than of a man.

Having arrived in the right neighbourhood, I now turned to the directions given in the note. While pretending to read the plaque in front of St Giles's Church, I looked all about me. I saw no uniforms, no greatcoats disguising inspectors with conspicuous moustaches, nor any other suspicious characters, unless one wishes to include Daft Dickie, the half-wit, who sits dangling his short legs over the railing round the church, as though he were superintending the renovations himself.

When I was certain that I had not been followed from Lothian Street, I found the bookshop and opened the door. Inside, the gloom discouraged customers from reading what they had not yet purchased. Among them, with a copy of Nicholas Culpeper's *Health for the Rich and Poor by Diet without Physick* open in his hands, I found Bell, his medical bag beside him, but otherwise not much changed from when we had parted.

"I believe the prime minister is seeing a certain Dr Joseph Kidd, an advocate of homoeopathy, the former owner of this weighty object." He blew dust from the top of the book when he had snapped it closed. Under the watchful eye of the proprietor, we went out of the shop.

"What is the name of the clerk we are seeking?"

"John James M'Dougal in the Board of Works,

Department of Finance." Together we crossed the High Street, working our way slowly through the drays and carriages. Already the light was beginning to give up on another autumn day, the shadows had started creeping from their hiding-places and re-establishing their hold on the heart of the city.

We entered the City Chambers, made a few enquiries and soon were sitting in chairs designated for people who had a grievance with their assessment. John James M'Dougal responded to the greeting I brought from his friend Hew M'Chesney, but he remained a busy man, not to be trifled with. His straight back was eloquent of his hopes of advancement. I introduced Dr Bell and Joe took up the questioning from that point. At once he improved upon my errors: his professional status was touched upon in passing. He demonstrated that, in spite of our introduction which came from the bar in The Wounded Stag, we were people of serious intent.

"We want to know what you can tell us about Gordon Eward," he said.

"Gordon Eward, is it? He's about to be revenged, is he not? Blood for blood. The Lord shall destroy the ungodly."

"That may well be, sir," said Bell, "but it is my belief that the wrong man may pay the price for Eward's foul murder. You can help us find the guilty party before it is too late." I could sense Bell taking on a new character. He had adopted an earnestness that matched M'Dougal's own.

"But, sir, I never met the woman, that … that … opera singer, Mlle Clery."

"That doesn't signify. We want to know about Eward as *you* knew him. What did he do in the Board of Works?"

"Why, he was a clerk like the rest of us. He audited the books of several departments because of his training as an accountant."

"Which departments?"

"He was responsible for Works, City Assessments, Board of Trade and Poor Law."

"Can you tell me who is in charge of these departments?"

"Of course I can. Graham Falconer is my chief here at Works, Archie Thornton is at Trade, O.L. Patterson is head of Poor Law Administration and, of course, Andrew Burnham has the heavy City Assessment responsibilities."

"Andrew Burnham. What relationship does he have to the Procurator-Fiscal?"

"Andrew is the third son of Sir William."

"Was he acquainted with Eward?"

"Professionally, they knew each other and worked together. Socially, their lives were vastly different, although Eward's family was not in any way inferior to Andrew's. Andrew was able, because of his father, to inhabit the world of polite society, whereas Gordon was always struggling."

"But he travelled to Menton, in the south of France. He attended the opera. He, no doubt, lavished gifts upon his mistress, Hermione Clery." Bell stated these facts as though they were in fact a question.

"Last year his father died, leaving him a small inheritance. Instead of investing it wisely, he had been using it to buy opera seats. It's a sore pronouncement on a man who was in every other way a practical man."

"Now, when Gordon Eward was so heinously murdered in his lover's nest, Mr M'Dougal, who picked up the traces left unattended in his office?"

"Why, it was Andrew Burnham. He was head of a department, but not Eward's chief."

"Inasmuch as we are speaking about a murder, it seems odd asking about 'usual procedures,' but was it usual for the head of another department to pick up the pieces after Eward's sudden and tragic death?"

"Tragic? It was nothing o' the kind! It was a judgment!"

"Nevertheless?"

"Andrew Burnham wanted to help out in the emergency. It was his right. The records of his department were being reviewed just then, so it was natural for someone who was familiar with these accounts to help to put them in order."

"I see, I see. Were these spending estimates? Future purchases? What sort of accounts were involved? You'll forgive a poor layman's ignorant questions, sir. I am simply trying to get a grasp upon these matters, so far from my poor consulting rooms and patients."

"The accounts involved, let me see, the accounts—"

"—are none of your business! M'Dougal, are you in the habit of admitting into the counting house every Tom, Dick and Harry who can navigate these halls? No offence is intended, gentlemen. But this enquiry is monstrously irregular! You have no business here! I must insist that you leave at once! M'Dougal, please return to your room." M'Dougal glanced momentarily at Bell, made a small animal noise, then took to his heels down the corridor, scattering a stack of paper registration forms in his wake. A door was heard to slam shut a long distance away.

TWENTY-FOUR

"Am I right in the belief that I am addressing Andrew Burnham, head of the City Assessment department?"

"What concern is that of yours, sir?"

"I see that I am right." This flustered the bureaucrat who now faced us with angry brows. While I stood mute, unable to find the words which would transform Burnham into an ally, Bell examined the man who stood before us. He was a well-dressed, not unhandsome young man with ginger-coloured hair, and an expression he could only have learned from his father. He was leanly built for his height, which must have been close to six feet, and carried himself in a self-assured manner, as he had just demonstrated. He was wearing a well-brushed fashionably dark coat, as though he had been on his way out when he learned of our seeking out John James M'Dougal. For some reason, he looked familiar: then I remembered the group of drunken young men who had accosted Graeme Lambert and me coming out of Rutherford's bar.

Bell introduced himself to Burnham and then, indicating me, calmly made my name known to the young bureaucrat, who was controlling his anger with a firm grip. "We are desperately seeking all the help we can get for young Lambert. You see, it is only a matter of hours. You are someone who could render us incalculable assistance. We understand the breach in your management practices that this entails, but when a life is at stake..."

"You are the Dr Bell who has been questioning people? The one who is wanted for questioning in the murder of

Inspector Webb?"

"I am, indeed, sir. And I will gladly surrender myself to the authorities as soon as I have either saved young Lambert or failed to beat the hangman in his lethal work. You, sir, if you choose, can help us as no other."

"This is not only highly irregular, it is quite outside the law. In helping you, I should be as guilty as you are."

"Sir, I promise you that I will surrender myself into your hands as soon as we have succeeded or failed. No matter. I am ready to face the consequences. Perhaps my friend Doyle will join me in that promise. What could be fairer? What more could you wish?"

"Mr Burnham," I said, "I have heard that you are a sporting gentleman. Here is sport royal, if you are game. You have our assurances that succeed or not, we will end our struggle right here, or where you will. Remember, the murdered man was a colleague of yours." Burnham looked from Bell to me and back again. For a long time he said nothing.

"You say he was a colleague. Gordon Eward was more than that, he was a friend."

"Then you'll help?"

"I will do what I can. I have no wish to see an innocent man die, if innocent he be. Wherein may I help you?"

"Splendid!" shouted Bell. "Splendid! You knew the man well?"

"We were locked up in the same counting house for many years. I shared his love of music and many times we visited the concert hall together. We had invented accounting techniques that tended to ease the burden of our work. He was clever with figures, Dr Bell, but..."

"Yes?"

"He was too clever by half. I don't know why he needed the money. I don't know when he began—"

"What are you saying, man?"

"I had to straighten out the mess he left behind him. There were discrepancies in his books, funds missing, withdrawals that remained uncovered. Then, too, I found that he had invested heavily in the Firth of Tay Bridge Company. Great profits will come in time, but the bridge has only been open sixteen months."

"You discovered this? Who else knows?"

"I made my findings available to the Procurator-Fiscal directly."

"Your father. And what did Sir William decide to do about it?"

"The missing sums were calculated and assessed. Because of the suddenness of his death, because of the police enquiry, it was decided to cover the missing funds from other departments that had been showing a better balance than had been expected. The amount of missing money was considerable, as I have said, but in that I am speaking in terms understood by you and your friend here. As a missing portion of our total tax revenues, the monies unaccounted for amounted to a pittance. I am speaking of under two hundred thousand pounds. The budget of my own department totals several times that amount. In covering the loss we acted as Lloyd's of London acted at the time of the Langham scandal: we chose to cover the missing money and allow the poor, desperate murdered man to be buried with no blot upon his memory. It was an act of charity."

"Who else knows of this?"

"The chief constable and the deputy chief, Mr M'Sween. Perhaps Inspector Webb knew. I don't know about that."

"But no one else here is aware of the steps you initiated? Not even the clerk M'Dougal we were just questioning?"

"Certainly not! What we did was bend policy in order

to react in a humane and Christian way to a situation that is unlikely ever to arise again. Irregular it was, as so it remains, but, damn it, sir, I would do it again!"

"And it does you credit, Mr Burnham. Have you, by any chance, any information of Mlle Clery's husband, Mario Cabezon?"

"I had no idea the woman was married at all."

"She was indeed. The husband lives in Dewar Place, no great distance from the house where the murders were done."

"I heard nothing of this in reports of the trial."

"A small omission, Mr Burnham, among so many. But, let me not keep you longer. There is still much to do and time is winging onward. Come, Doyle. We have not a second to lose."

"Dr Bell? I release you from the promise you made in this room. And I wish you success in your quest. God speed!"

In less than twenty minutes we had made our way through The Lawnmarket, along Johnston Terrace, under the eminence of the Castle to the west end of the city. Dewar Place was a fine example of the New Town's Georgian architecture, only diminished by having the railway cut through the corner of the street. The address had been fashionable. Indeed it remained marginally so at the south end, but where the city directory indicated the address of Sr Mario Cabezon, the block was encrusted with the grime of forty years of railway traffic. Nevertheless, under the green discolouration of his brass plaque, the name

Sr Mario Cabezon
formerly of La Scala, Milan
teacher of voice
2nd Floor

could be easily seen. The stairs leading to the door were

bracketed with a curved balustrade, much damaged by soot, and the door appeared to have had its locks changed rather often over the last ten years or so.

Inside, the smells of cooking and the fires of early autumn made the climbing of the stairs unpleasant. The splendid curve of the staircase seemed to add to the look of genteel poverty rather than detract from it. The door on the second floor, with a pasteboard card pinned to the wall beside it, looked sturdy and untouched by the general dilapidation evident elsewhere.

The pounding of my friend's stick against the door brought footsteps in our direction. When the door was opened, after the unfastening of several locks, the location of the head in the new-opened space was something of a shock. It was a good head below where one expected to find it. The man could not have been taller than five foot one or two. It was a pleasant face, but with worried dark eyes, deep-set in an angular arrangement of features. His hair was jet-black and glossy, his brow high, and his whole figure conspired to make him appear taller than he actually was. He wore a brace upon his left leg.

"I am Sr Mario Cabezon, gentlemen. Whom have I the honour of addressing?" He said this with no trace of accent that I could detect. With the fiery looks that seemed appropriate to the voice teacher, the voice was badly matched. It belonged to another vocal cliché, that of the bankers of Charlotte Square among others. Of course, when I thought about it, it was only natural for someone sensitive to nuances of accents to begin remedial work with himself. As he backed away from the door, allowing us to penetrate into the main room of the apartment, I could see that he had imitated Scots bankers successfully in other areas as well: the furnishings of the room, from the large pianoforte near the windows to the gilt mirrors, the hangings, the rugs, everything suited an establishment of a man, if not of high fashion, at least one of comfortable conservative taste, with possessions which a curator of the art and furnishings of the last century would not be ashamed to call his own.

Bell introduced us and explained our mission. We were invited to sit on a couch that seemed to have been inspired by Hepplewhite or Sheraton. A black servant appeared and vanished only to return in a few minutes with cups and a tea tray. As soon as we were settled, and long before refreshments arrived, we were asked by our host:

"Gentlemen, how may I help you?"

"Sr Cabezon," began Bell, "forgive me for asking, but how does an Italian teacher of voice, in the middle of Edinburgh, come to bear a Spanish name?"

"Ah! Do you want a treatise on the twists and turns of the branches of my family tree, or will the explanation that my family has been Italian since the Renaissance suffice? A distant connection was a pupil of Il Perugian, the painter."

"It was idle curiosity and I apologize to you."

"Not a word of it, Dr Bell. I am surprised that you recognized the origins of the name. I'm a distant relation of a sixteenth-century Spanish musician."

"Yes, the blind organist they call 'The Spanish Bach.' More to the point, Sr Cabezon, have you been visited before by the police investigating the death of your late wife?"

"I was interviewed and questioned by a police inspector called Bryce about two weeks after Hermione was killed."

"No further contacts from the official police?"

"None whatever. I would have thought that, as the husband of one of the victims and a natural enemy of the other, they would have had me in their cells as soon as the crime was discovered."

We each took a cup from Sr Cabezon as he poured it. It somehow suited the setting. Powdered periwigs could hardly have improved matters.

"What contact had you with Mlle Clery since she came to the city?"

"Why, none at all. She had me bound over to keep the peace last year in London. I assumed that the judgment operated north of the Tweed as well as in the south."

"And you accepted this?"

"No. Not at once. Certainly not. But there is a building-up of data that at last informs even the most stubborn of fools: the woman no longer delights in your company. The idea takes hold in the end and one gets on with his life."

"But, you continued to follow her!"

"I continued to follow the opera, sir. My livelihood depends upon the lyric stage. I follow this company because I have long-established connections in the company. My dear departed wife may have flattered herself that I pursued her; the pedestrian truth is that I have been following my trade. It is a gypsy life, Dr Bell. I will away again when the opera company completes its season, barring the accident of a flood of pupils from this city."

"Yet I see, signor, from the banker's boxes against the wall—so out of place in a room like this—that you are not altogether the gypsy you seem to be."

"Ah, yes, you have discovered my little vice. I dabble in stocks and shares. In a modest way. I'm no Baring, I assure you. I have some consols which may eventually amount to something. In the meantime, I do not entertain lavishly."

"May I enquire more precisely about these securities, signor?"

"As you please. But I don't see the relevance." Cabezon got up from his chair and went over to the banker's boxes

and lifted the tin lid. He called out the names of companies
we had heard of and others that I for one had no knowledge of at all. Only one name caught my ear. I had heard it
spoken of so recently: the Firth of Tay Bridge Company.

"I have ten thousand shares," admitted the singing
teacher.

"May I ask how you heard of them, Sr Cabezon?"

"Talk in the Green Room at the opera. I can say with certainty that Hermione never mentioned them. She wouldn't
have known a share from a sachet, Dr Bell."

"I see, I see. Could you give me the name of your broker, signor? I might take a plunge myself." Cabezon wrote
a name on a scrap of lined staff paper and passed it over.
Bell glanced at it for a second before putting it safely away
in an inner pocket.

"Do you believe, Sr Cabezon, that Alan Lambert murdered both Mlle Clery and her inamorato?"

"What am I to believe? I never met the man. The law
says he did it. What am I, a poor teacher of music, to do
but believe what I am told. In whose interest would it be to
punish an innocent man?"

"In whose interest indeed," said my friend.

TWENTY-FIVE

On leaving Sr Cabezon, we walked back to the house where the crime was committed. It reconfirmed in my mind that it was a short jaunt from the home of the seemingly guiltless husband to that of his murdered wife. How much weight should be given to Cabezon's bland confession that it was a case of "all passion spent"? I asked Bell about this as we walked, head down and with long strides:

"'Husbands are in heaven whose wives scold not,'" he said. "It's too bland, too bloodless for me to accept, Doyle. If he was ever in love with her, can she have killed that emotion in him so utterly? Can she have become such a matter of indifference? My knowledge of these things begins to splinter and break. Nor do I expect you to be able to add greatly to my understanding. We are both of us out of our depth." He shook his head, went on muttering to himself and linked hands behind his back as we turned in to Morrison Street, casting about for a cab.

We had walked well nigh to West Port before we were able to stop a hansom. Bell instructed the driver to take us round to Lothian Street but to pass his door without stopping. As the cab came down the street, it was easy to see that the door was being watched. One dark-clad ruffian stood exactly where Webb's minion had formerly held the ground. Another two were placed nearer the house, each plain-clad man having adopted a stance that could not have fooled a backward child. Had the word "police" been attached to their coats, they could not have been more conspicuous. Bell gave the cabbie my address and the horse trotted off in that direction with a similar result.

"I would wager that the university and my own surgery are also well watched tonight, Conan. I think I have hit upon a way to arrange for our capture to satisfy the conditions that we settled in York. I begin to feel that the curtain to the last act in this tragedy is about to rise. I am rather interested in discovering how it will play."

"In the theatre, Doctor, it has always helped to have the script of the author to work from. Here we must make up our parts as best we can."

"Not entirely true, my friend. We have learned a great deal about this business in the past few weeks. And, of course, we know how the story ends." This statement so surprised me that my response must have been visible in my face long before I was able to give it utterance.

"You know the ending? You know who murdered Mlle Clery and her friend?"

"Of course. What do you think I am, a ninny? I dare say that you too could name the guilty party after reviewing what we have learned. And remember, you did much of the work yourself. I hardly stirred from my surgery or my study."

"Still, Doctor, I canna guess the name of the guilty party," I said, sliding, in my excitement, into broad Scots.

"And when I have told you, you will say 'How obvious! How could anyone say otherwise?' You observe, my friend, you even see, which is better than most so-called observers, but you do not allow yourself to be led by the facts to the only possible set of circumstances that will explain all parts of this intriguing puzzle."

"Puzzle? Is that all it is to you, sir? A puzzle? An entertainment like a game of chess or a mathematical problem?"

"To see well, Doyle, you must see clearly. To do that, you must shun anger and habits of thought. Assume nothing. You or I could be the guilty party until we have been logically eliminated. Any of the people we have met could have done the deed. That they did not must be demonstrated in every case."

"Where are we going now?" I asked, not knowing how to respond, nor how to tease from the doctor an answer to the question burning on my lips.

"All will be revealed in good time," he said, and that was the last word on the subject until he surprised me again. This time, it was a word to the cabbie, not to me: "Driver, take us to the office of Donald Webster in North Bank Street." He was reading from the paper Cabezon had given him. I waited in the cab, while Bell disappeared into the small, rather dusty office with a shingle waving to the left of the door. He was gone less than ten minutes. From the broker we went to the office of Henry Burgoyne in the Grassmarket. Here we waited at the curb until a messenger came running down the street and almost, but not quite, past the door. He went inside and came out again in less than two minutes holding a bright sixpence in his hand. Now both of us got out, but kept the hansom waiting.

Burgoyne, it turned out, was an officer in the Firth of Tay Bridge Company. Bell told me this while we waited for a wee slip of a girl to inform her employer that we had arrived.

"Mr Thompson and Mr Blanchard! Welcome, sirs, welcome! I have only this minute been informed that you were in the city and looking for an investment opportunity. Let me present my associate, David M'Clung." The face that came around the door-jamb belonged to the hatless fair-haired young man who had accosted Graeme Lambert and me on our way home from Rutherford's bar some nights ago. Hands were extended and shaken, the weather was apologized for, and we were politely manhandled into Burgoyne's *sanctum sanctorum*.

"Gentlemen, may I get you a wee dram of something

against the inclemency of the season?"

"That's very good of you, Mr Burgoyne, but unnecessary," said Bell in a deeper voice than I remembered him using before. "But you could furnish me and Mr Blanchard with a list of investors in the Tay Bridge venture."

"Ah-hah! The Firth of Tay Bridge Company! A venture, gentlemen, no longer. It has been in operation daily for more than a year. The risks, and there were many, are now buried in the past." After more palaver with the sleek and excited Mr Burgoyne and the agreeable Mr M'Clung, we were shown the list we had requested. After looking down the names included, Bell asked for a prospectus of the company and, with it in our possession, we made our way back to the cab. Burgoyne stood on his doorstep watching our retreat, wiping his forehead with a large red handkerchief. His partner joined him there. It was hard to see which of them was more surprised at the shortness of our visit.

"Next stop, Waverley Station," Bell sang out so that the driver could hear. "We have to meet the train from the south." He spoke as one who had committed Bradshaw's Monthly Railway Guide to memory. As he settled back in his seat, he looked at me, enjoying, I thought, my misery and confusion.

"My dear Doyle, we are watched for at every corner. All our haunts are being spied upon. I dare say even Rutherford's bar has a spy from the chief constable looking for us. What I mean to do, with your approbation, is to give ourselves up to the supreme authority in matters of life and death: we shall give ourselves up to the official whose function is the cutting of the thread of life itself. I am suggesting that we meet this train and surrender ourselves to Mr Marwood, the man from Horncastle."

"The hangman?" I asked, not believing my ears.

"The same," said he.

TWENTY-SIX

Waverley Station was crowded. Full of noise, steam, grit, the odour of tar and that strange sort of illumination that belongs chiefly to major railway terminuses. Bell examined the arrival schedule and purchased two platform tickets before we walked down the ways. The London train had just arrived and was disgorging its human cargo into the waiting arms of loved ones and relations.

"Come!" Bell urged and began moving towards the end of the train. "This last third-class car was added after the train was made up in London. Marwood boarded at Sheffield, after travelling from Horncastle to Lincoln, and from Lincoln to Sheffield. He would probably have gone into the emptier coaches. I believe it is usual with Marwood to trade his second-class ticket, supplied by the Home Office, for a third. A penny saved is a penny got, in his line of work."

"Do you know the man?"

"Few do. His acquaintances are notoriously short-lived. Ah, here is a possibility. Note the small satchel, and the retiring acolyte, a first-time assistant, or I miss my guess. His clothing comes from the Midlands. Ah, and he has just popped one of his famous boiled sweets into his gob. That settles it!"

The man Bell had singled out from among the alighting dozens was a middle-aged man, not unhandsome of countenance, although inclined to be ruddy. He wore an impressive watch-chain across his ample chest. His low felt hat, tidy black cravat and frock-coat gave a fleeting impression—a rather northern one—of the late Prince Consort. He shepherded his assistant, who carried an overnight case as though he had never been farther from home than the nearest market town: his eyes were blinking at the size of Waverley Station. Bell approached them and I followed.

"Mr Marwood, I presume," said Bell, tipping his hat.

"And if I am, to whom am I indebted for this unexpected welcome? If it *is* a welcome."

"Oh, you are most assuredly welcome to Edinburgh. And so is your assistant. My name is Bell, Dr Joseph Bell, and this is *my* assistant, Conan Doyle, who will soon be a medical man like myself."

"This here is Jack ... What are we going to call you, Jack?"

"Jack Dawes, Mr Marwood. It's not a bit like my real name and it's not difficult to remember." Marwood smiled at his assistant and then turned again to Dr Bell.

"Have you been sent by the governor of the gaol, sir?" Bell smiled and inclined his head in a manner that might be taken for a nod. Then Marwood turned to his assistant with an open smile: "You see that, Jack, they know how to greet a person in Scotland!" By now we were walking up the ways, surrendering our platform tickets at the gate, and making our way to the four-wheeler we had engaged.

As we walked, a third person slipped into step with us. Whether he had come from the train, I did not see, but he seemed to know Marwood and Bell took no notice of him. While we climbed aboard the carriage, the stranger flagged down a hansom that had just disembarked three young ladies, all dressed in mourning. When our coachman shook his horses into action, the hansom turned his black-and-white nag around and followed us at a modest distance.

"Gentlemen, perhaps you will not be surprised to hear that your most cordial welcome is not the greeting that is

often extended to someone of my trade. Not long ago, a
stranger in Norwich was thrown into a duck pond on the
general suspicion that he was myself. He took the leaders
of the mob responsible to court for assault and defamation.
Counsel for the defendant claimed that being called the
hangman could not possibly be defamatory, since the hangman, like a judge, performs an important civic function.
Unfortunately, the court ruled it was absurd to argue that
the executioner's office is a branch of the judiciary, and
awarded damages. In my view, gentlemen, the person of the
hangman, or executioner, as I prefer, is akin to that of the
judges, magistrates and justices in the land, whatever a
Norwich judge says. It is fearfully hard to see that even the
judge that condemns a man to the gallows holds himself
aloof from the unpleasant task he sets upon other shoulders. It is most vexing." From time to time, Marwood
popped a peppermint into his mouth. Each time, he offered
the bag to all comers before putting it back into one of the
huge pockets on the side of his coat. He remarked upon the
sharp cold turn the weather had taken. Jack Dawes looked
at me with suspicion I could not shake off. After a time, he
turned to look at the view.

Bell began to quiz the hangman about his travels. He
asked if he had often been to Scotland. In uncharacteristic
hyperbole he began lauding the excellence of Scottish ale.
We quickly discovered that Marwood considered himself a
connoisseur of good ale. Before I was quite aware of what
was happening, it had been concluded that we would stop
at The Beak's Wig to taste of the best Scottish brews. Marwood, despite the blue ribbon of a total abstainer worn
prominently on his lapel, was much amused and entranced
by the suggestion. The ribbon, I took it, was not intended
seriously in his present company so far from Horncastle and
Lincolnshire. With hardly a look at his watch, he gave both

ears to Joe Bell's history of the drinking establishments of Rose Street. I had no idea that such lore formed part of my friend's vast store. He pointed out where, in former times, prostitutes sold their wares; where "Half-Hangit Maggie" used to tell of her amazing resurrection; and, turning in at a well-used door, where Burke and Hare used to drink away their ill-gotten money.

"They were businessmen, providing dead bodies for Dr Knox's dissection classes, Mr Marwood. In this tavern, Burke and Hare divided the spoils of their necrophagous trade. They began by delivering corpses they came across in the wynds and closes, or resurrected from Greyfriars cemetery. Later, they provided freshly dead specimens of their own making. Very profitable they found it. The notorious Dr Knox was liberality itself, Mr Marwood. You don't know how difficult it is to get a cadaver that isn't pocky even nowadays."

All of this Marwood and his young assistant absorbed as though they had never fallen in with better companions than ourselves.

In the *howff*, Bell ordered ale by the half-measure, so that Marwood would be able to savour the difference from one to the next. "Now this, my friends, is a dark, nut-brown ale made in small quantity for a titled Highland family. I happen to know that, apart from a small stock that comes here, a practice that comes of a service done during the Forty-five, involving a Jacobite lass and her Georgian lover, this ale is unknown except among knowl-edgeable people. Ah, but the next, the next may be called the king of ales. This has won prizes at international exhi-bitions in Copenhagen, Munich and Chicago. It was award-ed medals at the Great Exhibition...!" And so he went, on and on, with Marwood and his associate drinking glass after glass with evident enjoyment. A mellower Marwood could not be imagined. He drank deeply and commented intelligently upon each glass. He introduced us to a comic song from the English music halls in which his name figured prominently.

"Here's another one, gentlemen," he said, half getting to his feet. "This question was asked at the Palladium in London: 'Tell me, if Pa killed Ma, who'd kill Pa?' You know the answer to that? I bet you don't. The answer is: 'Marwood!'" At this, he dissolved in a broad, bluff laugh that breathed a beery sort of sweetness and light into every corner of the *howff*.

"Mr Marwood, perhaps you will have heard of my Irish colleague, the Reverend Samuel Haughton, MD, FRS, and a Fellow of Trinity College, Dublin. He has written a small treatise on the subject of hanging, from a mechanical and physiological point of view."

"I remember seeing that. Has some very difficult sums in it; calculations with fractions, square roots and so on. I try to keep my arithmetic simple. I'll leave the x, y and z for the reverend gentleman. You have to watch them Irish: they're all up to summat. I remember one time in Kilmainham Gaol…" Marwood was launched on an anecdote with an Irish locale. This was followed by other stories with settings all over the British Isles. Each was the tale of death on the scaffold. And yet we laughed to hear Marwood tell it.

Bell introduced the hangman and his friend to more ales and porters, all the while keeping up a commentary which touched upon the strengths of each of the proffered brands. I had early stopped trying to match them drink for drink. Otherwise, even with my student's head for alcohol, I should have fallen into the sawdust on the floor and slept for some hours. As far as I could see, Joe and the man from Horncastle were drinking gill for gill, sometimes crooking their arms around one another. After some time, Marwood's features seemed to be subsiding into the lower portion of his face as his eyes grew heavy and their lids closed from time to time. As for Jack Dawes, the assistant, his eyes had closed much earlier. He was now slumped on his bench and oblivious to further pain or pleasure.

"Ah, my friend," said Joe to the hangman, "it is strange that you should come all this way to Scotland just to taste of its ale. We are a whisky-drinking people. There's more than one thing to do with malt than brew it. Have you had a sip of the finest distillation known to man? I am speaking of a blend of heather from the shaws and peat from the glens. The savour of it alone is enough to turn a rational, sober man into a prophet, a poet, a rhapsodizer on the themes of love and life and beauty. Mr Marwood, I am speaking of the single malt. It is a creature you seldom see where you come from. Aye, they call it by the name of whisky south of the border, but it is not the thing itself. But let me show you the way. In after times you will remember the poor doctor who put your foot on the ladder leading to Elysium..." He brought the landlord close and ordered with great charm and ceremony a dram of the finest whisky in the house. When it arrived, we all—all but young Dawes—lifted our glasses in a toast to the visitors from the south. The executioner responded with a pledge to our civility and courtesy. When the drinks were gone and the glasses were emptied, Marwood was beginning to look decidedly off-colour. He suddenly moved the table back with his belly and stood to attention. For a moment, I thought that he was going to propose another toast, but no, he was simply trying to move past the sleeping form of his companion in order to find the lavatory. He stumbled through the crowded room, twisting, upsetting a chair or two, in the direction I had indicated. As soon as he was gone, Bell was on his feet:

"Quick, Doyle. There's not a moment to lose. Take the

smaller bag!" I could see that he had pulled the dark valise belonging to the hangman from the floor and was making for the front of the *howff*. At the door, he paid the reckoning and in less time than it takes to say it, we were back reeling in the twilight of Rose Street running down towards Hanover Street. Here Bell hailed a cab, and a moment later we were settled back into the leather cushions breathing heavily. Joe was the first to speak, but he did not do so until he had looked from the cab to see if we were being followed.

"Well, well, my friend. You have just witnessed a side of my nature the existence of which I would have doubted two hours since. You have also witnessed the Bell variation on the classical method of arsenic poisoning."

"Poisoning! Dr Bell, I must pro—"

"The variation is harmless, Conan. Rest assured. In the classic recorded cases, such as that of the Marquise de Brinvilliers, poisoning over a long period of time using arsenic is brought to a head by the administration of antimony. In my variation, a prolonged period of drinking ale to excess is brought to a sudden conclusion by a change to hard spirits. I have often entertained the theory of its effectiveness but never imagined that I would ever be able to give it a practical trial. How is your head?"

"Swimming. But, I confess, more from recent events than from the drink."

"I hope you noticed that I was spilling a good deal of my drink under the table."

"Where it mixed with my own. But why, Doctor? Why did we do it? Why did we make the hangman drunk? He will be well enough in the morning to see to young Lantbert. His headache may be severe, but he will still be able to do his duty."

"And with what will he do it, lad?"

"Why...why..." Here my eyes fell for the first time on the two grips we had taken from the southerners. I looked up at Bell for a further word.

"You canna hang a man without your rope, Conan. You canna tie his arms and feet without your straps nor cover his head without a county kerchief. We have borrowed his bag of tricks. Call it insurance. We have bought some time. We have scotched the snake, not killed it."

TWENTY-SEVEN

Before driving north to Leith, where Bell had taken rooms at an inn under assumed names, he had the driver take him through the city where he left calling cards at some of the finest Georgian doors. Each card contained a hastily scrawled message which required the receiver's attendance the following morning at the New City Gaol. At dawn, shortly before the appointed hour for Alan Lambert to make his last confession and prepare to walk to the gallows, Bell and I, after a rough night, stopped to awaken Lieutenant Bryce and brought him along in the four-wheeler. On our arrival, we banged on the tall, thick, double doors of the gaol. The two bags belonging to Marwood and his assistant we left in the care of the cabbie who was asked to wait for us. As we stood at the door, a second cab came along. From it alighted the stranger from the station: a well-dressed, self-assured man of middle age.

As soon as a warder opened the small door set in the larger double doors, we requested to be brought at once to the governor of the gaol, where Bell introduced himself and his companions. The stranger was introduced simply as Mr Wilson, from London. While the governor, one Major Ross, exchanged dark looks with Bryce, he appeared to be deeply displeased with the rest of us as well.

"You've made a sorry mess of this, Dr Bell. You've lost your position of trust at the university for this prank, I warrant. I only hope that you have had the decency to bring with you the necessary equipment—purloined by you—so that I may do my duty as I have sworn to do. You have proven yourself to be a most dangerous clown, sir, and I cannot but rejoice in your fall."

"That's as may be, Major," said Bell. "I take it that the execution has not yet occurred?"

"It has been postponed for an hour and will, by God, take place at nine o'clock without any further hitch or delay. Your meddling has won you nothing, sir. You have simply given serious distress to a brave young man who was prepared to die like a man until you unsettled him. He has won the respect of every man within these walls. He would have taken his punishment like a soldier, sir, until you interfered."

"Yes, it's very edifying for all when the victim smiles and shakes hands, isn't it? Too bad you couldn't have trained him to stick his head in the noose like Punch does to Jack Ketch. I trust that Mr Marwood is here and has found something to soothe his sore head."

"Dr Bell, I will not banter with you. If you have something to say, then say it and be gone. This is a busy day for me."

"Major Ross, I have been so bold as to invite certain people who have knowledge of this case to come here this morning."

"You had no right. The number of official witnesses has been made up. You must leave here at once."

"Perhaps not quite at once. I did not invite people here to witness an execution, but to prevent one."

"Then your hopes are doomed to disappointment, sir. I shall do my duty if I have to hoist him up myself. This is one of Her Majesty's gaols, sir, not a court of appeal."

"A court of appeal here in your office! What an extraordinary idea, Major. How neat, how tidy, how apt!"

"What are you maundering on about, Doctor?"

"Major Ross, I will not tease you further. Mr Wilson,

whom I just introduced to you, is the senior Queen's messenger. He is empowered to convey a message directly by telegraph to the Home Secretary. He is here this morning at the express wish of the prime minister to see that we conduct ourselves in a manner that will bring no further disgrace upon the name of justice in these islands." All eyes turned to Wilson, who hadn't moved. He stood stock-still, with the whisper of a smile on his lips.

"Sir, is this true? Can one believe this man?"

"It is true, Major. But be it understood that I am here to see that justice is done, not to make any judgments. I am a referee, plain and simple."

"Do you mean to say that we are going to try Lambert all over again here and now?"

"I mean to demonstrate his innocence. If I succeed in convincing you, then you will instruct the messenger yourself."

"And if you fail?"

"Ah, but I shall not fail, sir. First, may I ask you if there are among the witnesses assembled inside any who were involved in the trial?"

"Aye. The Lord Advocate, Sir George Currie, is here, acting in place of the sheriff of Midlothian, who, as you may know, is seriously ill. Mr Veitch is with his client now, taking his leave of him."

"Capital! Then both the defence and the prosecution are represented. You will note that, Mr Wilson. Major Ross, I suggest that these gentlemen be sent for." At almost the same moment a clamour began at the door as it was rapped upon loudly by a heavy-headed stick or club.

In ten minutes the large office of Major Ross was stuffed full of the people who knew most about the case of the murders in Coates Crescent. Sir George Currie, in fine form, tried to match the impatience of Major Ross. The

Lord Advocate is not to be trifled with! Adam Veitch
looked intrigued. Burnham, the Procurator-Fiscal, was in a
towering rage, until he was mollified by Ross, who
explained about the Queen's messenger. The new face
belonged to the chief constable, Sir Alexander Scobbie, a
giant of a man, now blighted and bent, as though struck by
lightning, and supporting himself cautiously with two
sticks. His deputy chief, Keir M'Sween, a broad-faced,
dark-eyed vigorous man in his forties, gave no indication
that we had once before met within these walls. Others in
the crowded room were Mlle Clery's forgotten husband,
the voice teacher Mario Cabezon, as well as the Procurator-
Fiscal's own son, young Andrew Burnham. Sitting somewhere near me was Graeme Lambert, the man who first
brought Bell into the case. The grey-haired gentleman next
to him, with fine grey gloves folded in his lap, could only
be his father.

When the doors had been shut by me at a cue from Bell,
he began to speak. He chose his words carefully and after
a nervous minute or two sank into his usual lecture theatre
manner that I knew so well. In spite of themselves, those
assembled in the panelled room, and even, it seemed, the
white plaster-cast heads of executed felons on the mantel,
turned to hear what Dr Bell had to say.

"Gentlemen, I will try to be brief. I came here this
morning to demonstrate the innocence of Mr Veitch's
client, Mr Alan Lambert, before the question of his innocence or guilt becomes an academic question. Here, in the
very shadow of the gallows, I have invited you to examine
evidence that a miscarriage of justice is scheduled to take
place this morning. I hope to be able to save, not only the
life of an innocent man, but the good name of British
justice from disrepute.

"To begin with, Alan Lambert's name first came into

this case because of a pawn-ticket he owned on a diamond brooch. That brooch, according to the ticket and the pawn-broker, had been in continuous pawn for some weeks prior to the crime. It could not have been the brooch that was taken from Coates Crescent on the night of the murders."

"It was my mother's brooch!" offered Graeme Lambert. "An heirloom given to Alan by my mother when my father would no longer assist him." The man sitting next to him said nothing, acquiescing with a bowed head.

"This false identification of the brooch led the police to Alan Lambert. There is nothing else to connect Lambert to either of the murder victims."

"There were several eye witnesses who gave testimony," suggested Keir M'Sween, the deputy chief.

"Good! Let us look at these eye witnesses. They came in response to the offer of a reward for information leading to the arrest of the criminal. Two hundred pounds, gentle-men, which has long since been paid out. When you look at these eye-witness descriptions, they bear no relation at all to the accused. They contradict one another about his size, his features and every aspect of his clothing. It recalls the Wilkhaven Ferry murder case of 1875 all over again. In that case, you will remember, Detective-Lieutenant Bryce demonstrated conclusively the danger of giving too much weight to paid witnesses.

"And let us look closer at these same witnesses. With-out going into detail this morning, let me remind you that many of them had either seen a photograph of the accused before they confirmed their identification, or they had seen him in the flesh in a New York jail under guard and in manacles. Those who know anything of police procedure will see the folly of this sort of identification. It is not strong enough to hang a man.

"At the trial, the Lord Advocate told the jury that he

would show that the accused knew of the jewellery in the possession of Mlle Hermione Clery. In the four-day record of the trial, he demonstrated no such connection. Yet, in his summation, he mentioned it again as though it had in fact been given in the evidence. Even the learned judge spoke of it as though it was part of the record. The Lord Advocate did his best to impute to the accused all sorts of wrong-doing, most of it without foundation. I have counted at least five and twenty errors in fact in his summation."

"All of this was gone into at the commissioners' hearing. You are beating a dead horse, Doctor." This from the Lord Advocate himself.

"Interesting point. More interesting is the fact that the commissioners were forbidden under their terms of reference to go into the conduct of the trial. Imagine, if you will, a commission that was so bracketed in absurdity that it was prevented from re-examining all of the evidence. One might as well set up a commission to examine an allegedly serious matter without giving it the power to name the wrongdoers when their identity becomes known."

"The man is plainly a lunatic. Major, I can stop here no longer!"

"I think you may be able to assist the interests of justice, sir, if you will be kind enough to tarry a few minutes longer." This from Wilson, who spoke in a level, calm voice that had the desired effect, for Sir George retained his seat. Perhaps it was Wilson's use of the somewhat literary word "tarry."

"None of what has been mentioned here this morning was re-examined! To make matters worse, the commissioners had the assistance of the Procurator-Fiscal and the chief constable, acting through his deputy. The defendant was neither heard from nor allowed to attend either in person or through representation. Surely the dice of justice have never been so unfairly loaded. The opportunity to set matters to rights, which was prompted by Detective-Lieutenant Bryce's letter to the Home Secretary, was scuttled. Bryce was destroyed for rocking the boat."

"Is this so?" asked Sir Alexander Scobbie, the ailing chief constable. "I don't recall any part of it."

"There was no need to set matters aright," explained his assistant. "We had our man and he knew we had him."

"What you mean is, you had spent so much in your absurd chase after this man that you were too embarrassed to admit that you had been on a wild-goose chase. Once you had the pawn-ticket and heard that Lambert had left the city, you thought that you had found your criminal in full flight: the murderer is fled to Liverpool, fled to New York! Oh, it was all highly dramatic, sending your officers and the eye witnesses across the Atlantic. But, any examination of the evidence explodes the idea that Lambert fled the city because of the crime. He had sold his larger possessions, concluded business arrangements, disposed of his lease, said farewell to a number of friends beginning weeks before the crime. The Lord Advocate spoke of flight, of haste when there was neither. What the Crown was trying to hide, and this to protect the law enforcement branch, was the fact that a great deal of money had been spent in pursuing the wrong man.

"How is he the wrong man? You, sir," Bell said, addressing the Lord Advocate, "told the court that Lambert could produce not a single witness who could place him anywhere but at the flat of Mlle Clery at the time of the murders. In fact, there were two witnesses who stated that he was at home eating his supper at that hour. You chose to suggest that they were prostitutes in league with the defendant. But there were independent witnesses who saw Lambert in his usual haunts in his own part of town

before and after he had that supper, but they were not
called.

"It is a serious matter in the administration of justice
when the police fail to provide the Crown with the full list
of their witnesses and their written precognitions. It is
equally serious when the Crown fails to disclose this material to the defending advocates. The state has greater power
than an individual, it must not use it to turn justice into a
travesty."

"M'Sween, tell me he is mad, sir!" demanded the chief
constable.

"Yes, I am mad. Mad as they use the word in the Grassmarket. Maddened to learn of public servants who treat the
public to short weights. Maddened to hear that Keir
M'Sween knew that Inspector Webb was taking active
steps to ensure that none of this would come out. The
pawnbroker and his wife were intimidated, so was the
hotel clerk from telling anyone that Lambert signed his
own name to the register in the Liverpool hotel on his
'flight' from justice. Aye, and when Detective-Lieutenant
Bryce brought this to the attention of the authorities, he
was not broken to the ranks, he was drummed out of the
service of which he was the chief ornament for so many
years."

"This is outrageous! I will not hear another word! Who
is this upstart? I am Sir William Burnham. I am nobody's
fool, certainly not yours!" For a brief moment, I thought
that the Procurator-Fiscal was rallying to our side, but I
was mistaken. It was an attempt to overturn the proceedings, but a lame one, for by now even Major Ross would
have hushed him where he stood, red in the face and
blustering.

"Gentlemen…" It was Mr Wilson. "I have heard
enough of this case to reach the conclusion that if an

injustice has not been committed, it is giving all the appearances of one. Consequently, I am about to telegraph the Home Secretary to order a stay of execution in this case. I will at the same time inform the Lord Provost of my action."

"You mean Alan will not be hanged?"

"Not this morning, young man. That much is certain." At these words, Graeme Lambert took his father in his arms. For some time father and son held one another in a tight embrace, Graeme's shoulders heaving with emotion. In spite of the older man's gravity and reserve, he did not try to prevent this show of emotion in public. In fact, he, himself, was seen to have tears running from his cheeks to his collar.

TWENTY-EIGHT

An hour later, the condemned man had been informed of the respite which the Home Office had telegraphed. He had been moved out of the condemned cell where he had spent the days since the trial.

The gathering in Major Ross's office had now been augmented by two. Marwood and his assistant had slipped in unrecognized by most of those assembled. Ross had been prepared to offer a stimulant—presumably purchased to stiffen the sinews of faint-hearted witnesses to Lambert's hanging. When some of those assembled resisted the idea of spirits at such a matutinal hour, tea was sent for and arrived in stoneware mugs on a tray. It proved to be strong and hot.

"And has the senior Queen's messenger now discharged his responsibilities?" asked Sir George Currie, the Lord Advocate, with the suggestion of a sneer. "Are we free to take up again the scattered traces of our lives and go from this place?"

"My official business is concluded. Nevertheless, I am bound to remain by curiosity, which I think might hold you for another quarter of an hour, sir."

"Of what should I be curious? You perhaps over-estimate my interest in this matter."

"That's as may be, but I for one am waiting for Dr Bell to conclude his story."

"Conclude it, he has only confused it. Now we must begin again to look for a new guilty party."

"The guilty party is in this room!" asserted Bell,

overhearing this exchange. "It will not take long to unmask him. Does that awaken your dormouse curiosity, sir?"

"Hrumph! I'll stay ten minutes, for want of other idleness." Bell cocked an eye and exchanged a glance with the Lord Advocate, as though they had suddenly something to share.

Bell began speaking again, with more assurance now, for the condemned man was at last safe from Mr Marwood's contrivances. Still, the thought of the murderer being among us excited the room unnaturally and was the cause of sly looks and suspicious glances among the company.

"When I was first approached by Graeme Lambert to save his brother from the gallows, I took the position that Lambert was innocent. The guilty party then was someone else, a Mr Guilty Party. I ruled out the possibility of it being a Miss Guilty Party or a Mrs Guilty Party because of the nature of the crime: two violent murders with a slashing blade done quickly one after the other. Still, even with women eliminated as a possibility, I was left with a notable puzzle. I had to ask myself, was Lambert also the intended victim of the murderer? Was his being brought into the crime part of a diabolical plot to murder *three* people? In the end, I discarded this theory. I commend it to some follower in the footsteps of the American writer, Mr Edgar Poe.

"The police have always assumed, and in this they were echoed by the newspapers, that Mlle Clery was the intended victim of the murderer. It is a natural assumption: she was a celebrated artiste, rich, famous and beautiful. Next to her, poor Eward was a little brown mouse: neither rich nor well known. His death has always been seen as an accident; had he not been in the Coates Crescent flat, he would not have shared Mlle Clery's fate. Or, had she another visitor that night, he, rather than Eward, would have had his throat cut. I was aware of the trap of this assumption, but for the moment I knew not what to do with it.

"The police have also said from the beginning that the motive for the crime was robbery. Now, gentlemen, this motive is absurd. Not that there weren't riches in jewels to be taken, but that in fact only one brooch was taken away. And whether that was taken by the murderer or by someone else who had access to the flat both before and after the crime has never been sufficiently looked into. If it was a robbery, what a remarkable robbery it was! There was no sign of a forced entry. All those locks and bolts up and down the door were each opened one after the other by one of the victims. And remember, there were two doors: a street door and the upstairs door to the flat. Both of them kept locked. So, the murderer was known to one of the victims.

"In a case of this kind, the murder of a woman and her lover, the police often find the spouse responsible. It is both tidy and it fits with what we know about human nature. In this case, Mario Cabezon, Hermione Clery's estranged husband, lived close to Coates Crescent. He had a motive: jealousy. In fact, he had been bound over to keep the peace. Had the authorities not been so invested in the pursuit of Lambert to Liverpool and New York, they would have seen this omission. Only the now-discredited Detective-Lieutenant Bryce saved the reputation of the force here: he alone questioned Mlle Clery's husband. As far as I know, no other policeman even knew that Mlle Clery had a living husband. I mention this, not to further add to the mounting list of police errors, but to demonstrate again the rash chase after the one 'fleeing' suspect.

"Is Sr Cabezon our murderer? I think not. If he were a taller man, more generously built around the shoulders, he might have done much, but he is shorter than both Eward

and Mlle Clery and with his leg brace in no way resembles
Webb's murderer, whom I saw outside Inspector Webb's
stairwell.

"Another thing that Bryce learned came from Mlle
Clery's agent, Tom Prentice, whom I have cabled in New
York. Prentice, Bryce learned, told Inspector Webb that the
maid, Hélène André, had visited him on the night of the
murders to tell him the news. She spoke of a man, *known
to her by sight*, whom she saw coming from the bedroom
and leaving the flat before the bodies were discovered. The
downstairs neighbour overheard peculiar noises above and
came to the door of the flat as the maid returned from a
trip to buy a newspaper. (A singular mission at that hour!)
He too stated that he saw a man coming out of the flat.
None of this is new. When Bryce learned of this he returned
to the station to see Prentice's precognition and that of the
maid. In both cases, the statements were full of omissions
signified by asterisks. The name of the man identified by
Hélène André was given as Mr XYZ. Surely, here we have
the murderer leaving the scene of the crime. Is this clue followed up? It is not. Why was the name of the suspect not
given in full? Many names come up in a criminal investigation. Such documents are seen only by the police officers
involved. Any need for anonymity surely arises at the
moment a case goes to trial: information is not normally
screened from the officers investigating the case. In this
instance, only the name of Mr XYZ was protected. When
I say protected, I choose the word with care. Both Inspector Robbie Webb and Detective-Lieutenant Bryce were
ordered to warn the witnesses involved not to repeat this
information.

"What, gentlemen, I ask you, might lead to such a happening? How often is a particular name lifted out of an
investigation and buried in secrecy—"

"Surely you are making too much of this, sir," interrupted the chief constable in a querulous voice. "You are imputing a serious irregularity if you continue along this road."

"Here, sir, are the facts. Judge of them yourself: Detective-Lieutenant Bryce has said that the senior officers investigating the case were told by their superior that *the movements of XYZ were strictly enquired into after the murder.* By whom, you might ask. Not by those closest to the investigation. The witness André later denied saying that she recognized XYZ at the commissioner's enquiry. Like the other witnesses at the enquiry, she was not under oath."

"Not under oath! I don't believe it!" This was the chief constable again. "I never heard of such a thing."

"Sir, your name appears as one of those involved in the daily proceedings of the enquiry. Are you saying that you don't remember this?"

"Doctor, there are so many of these enquiries. I canna get to all of them. And this one was held in such haste; a few days! M'Sween attended in my place. He was there as well as Sir William."

"Then perhaps you can explain, Chief M'Sween, how it was that after the witness André denied ever seeing XYZ and further denied that she ever said that she saw him, she was warned not to mention XYZ's name to anyone?"

"You have no business meddling in this thing, Doctor. You don't know what you are about. You wouldn't like me blundering into your operating theatre, I warrant you!" M'Sween was visibly turning red. Eyes that had been rooted on Bell moved to M'Sween's face.

"Answer the man's question, M'Sween. Clear this up for God's sake!" said the chief.

"And, while you are about it, tell us the name of Mr

XYZ. It was important enough to keep out of the murder investigation, and it most assuredly must have been a contributing cause to the murder of Robbie Webb."

"You meddling busybody!" shouted Keir M'Sween, getting to his feet and coming towards Bell. "You are undermining the fabric of the justice system! You are destroying in a moment what it has taken centuries to build! Will nothing satisfy you other than rendering the state helpless, returning it to chaos and anarchy?" Major Ross put a hand on M'Sween's arm, for otherwise he would have been at Bell's throat.

"Steady on, M'Sween," said Ross firmly, trying to push the officer into a chair. "We'll soon hear his answer. Well, sir," said Ross to Dr Bell, "the chief has levelled a serious charge at you. Do you intend anarchy? With what do you plan to replace the established institutions of law and order?"

"Major, a justice system, like a chain, is as strong as its weakest link. It works to no purpose if it does not work for all. Admittedly, the display of wigs and gowns in the High Court of Justiciary gives the appearance of dignity and solemnity and power to the system, but it is the day-to-day working of the system that is the substance behind the theatrical show. What we are facing, gentlemen, is an effort on the part of one man to manipulate that system, to let an innocent man go to his death rather than allow police and judicial errors to be made known. In addition to this, the system has been subverted to protect a multiple murderer. That, gentlemen, must not be allowed to happen."

Bell's unaccustomed eloquence stirred the people in Major Ross's office. Looks were exchanged; both Ross and M'Sween were looking uncomfortable, badly shaken in their principles.

"Sir," said the Lord Advocate, "what you have said is

no doubt a timely reminder of those precepts that should abide with every law officer of the Crown, and I thank you for putting your spur to any lapse in our sworn duties. Still, you have made only veiled accusations. If you have charges, bring them into court, make them known."

"Then, I will charge Keir M'Sween with using his high office to try to cover the traces of a silly and careless investigation, with keeping silent about facts that would have freed Alan Lambert of the charges against him, with failing to provide to either counsel or prosecution all of the records in the case, a small number of which would have given the prisoner then at the bar a speedy deliverance. There is more: he used Inspector Webb as his instrument to terrorize and intimidate witnesses to be silent, to change their precognitions and to try to stop Doyle and myself from uncovering the truth. He has had criminal knowledge in this matter from the beginning. I will not mention the pressure he brought to bear upon Doyle, here, and myself."

The room held its breath. The heavy mantel clock, with the mute plaster heads on either side of it, was the only sound. I myself was caught completely off-guard. Although I had been with my friend throughout the investigation, I had not expected this would be the result of our efforts. As soon as rational as well as irrational thought was possible, protests boomed out. The Procurator-Fiscal, his son, even Mr Veitch, whose bread one might have thought was buttered on the other side, shouted their objections to Bell's charges. Major Ross demanded that he substantiate his accusations at once. Again, all eyes, including my own, were on my friend.

"Chief M'Sween, will you make your office available to an independent search? I have not had the opportunity of seeing the pebble thrown into the water, but from the circular waves I can see where it struck. If the chief himself did not order Webb to intimidate witnesses, then it was you. You were Webb's superior officer. When Mr XYZ was *cleared*, as Bryce was told, it had to have been you who looked into his involvement, unless it was the chief."

"Look here, sir," said the old chief, "M'Sween has been carrying not only his own heavy and grave responsibilities, but, since my illness last year, most of mine as well. He is a capable, honest officer. He has helped, for very few shillings of the ratepayers' money, to make private and public property and these streets safe after dark. He is a dedicated and frugal officer. If I have my way, he shall have my post when I retire."

"What you are admitting, Chief, is that the force is hard-pressed and under-staffed. I make no argument against that. It is also under-financed. A good force is expensive. That is why M'Sween's chase after the 'fleeing' suspect is so heinous. It was wasteful. I suspect, sir, that you would have been more than a little critical to learn of M'Sween's blunder. It would have cost the force dear. Far better to have the culprit to show for the expense."

"Dash it all, Dr Bell, you're making a serious accusation, and I will support an independent investigation if only to prove that you are wrong," said the old chief. "You name any competent person to undertake such a search, and I will back you."

"What about Mr Andrew Burnham? He is a skilled administrator. He was able to detect the fiduciary irregularities in the accounts of Gordon Eward, the second murder victim. He helped to smooth away the irregularities in his books."

"What's this? I've never heard of such a thing!" said the Procurator-Fiscal, Sir William Burnham, with a sharp look at his son.

"Let me understand you, sir. Are you saying that

Gordon Eward's accounts were in disorder and that Andrew Burnham put them to rights with the connivance of the Procurator-Fiscal? This is insane! It wouldn't be condoned for a moment!"

"Sir Alexander, I take it that you were ignorant of Andrew's Good Samaritan gesture as well?"

"I certainly was. M'Sween, what do you know of this?"

M'Sween said nothing. He looked about to speak, but nothing could be heard. He was sweating so that his cheeks shone against the light.

"Doyle and I were told by Andrew himself that, with the blessing of the chief, the deputy chief and his father, the Procurator-Fiscal, Eward's pilfering from the accounts under his care was covered from departments that had not spent their budgets. The number he mentioned was just under two hundred thousand pounds."

"Two hundred thousand pounds!" echoed the chief with something of his old vigour. Sir William responded as well:

"This is as ridiculous as the rest of your rant, Dr Bell. What do you say for yourself, Andrew?"

"There were irregularities in Eward's books, which, in the circumstance of his sudden death, I managed to cover with funds from elsewhere. In speaking to an outsider, I thought it best to suggest that there was a general agreement that this should be done."

"This is most grave," said the old chief, Sir Alexander Scobbie.

"I felt I was merely replacing the divot so that others might play through," Andrew said directly to his father.

"Whatever your intentions were, my boy," said Sir Alexander, "you were quite wrong to do it. Charges may follow for all I know. Certainly it must be looked into."

"Sandy, you're addressing my son!" said the Procurator-Fiscal.

"You think I say it with an easy heart, Sir William? I do not."

"Unfortunately, fiduciary irregularities are only the smallest charges that are hanging over the head of Andrew Burnham," said Bell. "Unfortunately, I am convinced that he is also guilty of the three murders we have been looking into. Aye, the young man is guilty enough, clever enough and desperate enough."

Again Bell had achieved a sensation. Andrew Burnham's face went white. The men in the room looked from Burnham to Bell and back again. Of the two, they would have preferred young Burnham. He was of their sort, after all, but there was something about the accusation, despite its audacity, that made the room grow silent once more after Burnham and his father had sputtered their objections. We all wanted to hear what came next.

TWENTY-NINE

"Have you ever seen this note, Sir William?" Bell passed a piece of paper to the shaken father of Andrew Burnham. I recognized it as the sketch Bell had made of the note found in Webb's flat when we discovered his body. Sir William glanced at the paper, then let his arm fall, as though he had not the strength to compel it further. But something in it caught his attention, for he raised it again and studied it closely.

"The code words may be familiar to you from some time ago. I know it took me some days to recollect where I had seen them before. The drawings come from official staves held by county officials on ceremonial occasions in some English counties. The markings are runes going back to the Danes who introduced this clever sort of portable almanac. You may remember that the staff is called the Staffordshire Clogg. You come from Staffordshire, I believe, sir?"

"Aye, I come from there and I am familiar with the Staffordshire Clogg. You can see it in Camden's *Britannia* in a good library."

"Then you know that these little pictures represent dates, or more correctly, the name days of certain saints. St Crispian, patron of cobblers, is represented by two soles and so on. The note which was sent to Webb is signed by a diagonal cross. Have you any idea of what that might represent?"

"Why don't you kill me all at once and forgo this torture, Dr Bell? We both know what it means." The

Procurator-Fiscal allowed the hand with the paper in it to fall to its full length, as though the message had been written in lead.

"Yes, the cross of St Andrew. After the letters 'Yrs,' which I take to mean 'Yours' as in 'Yours sincerely,' the complimentary closing of the note, the cross follows. This is the signature: 'Andrew.'" The note was picked up from Sir William's limp hand and passed to the old chief.

"St Crispian, that is the Battle of Agincourt, the great victory of Henry V over the French knights, about a century after Bannockburn."

"The date was 25 October, 1415. In the context of the note, the date is given October 25 minus 2, or 23 October, gentlemen, which is today. 'Troubles over 23 October...' That is, I believe, a reference to what was to have taken place here this morning: the execution of Alan Lambert. The second symbol, that axe-head-like figure, stands for St Mary Magdalen, whose feast is celebrated on 22 July. 'Plans of 22 July less 1 well concluded.' What happened on 21 July?"

"Need you ask? That was the date of the first two murders," said Major Ross, who was certainly on top of the facts. "Mlle Clery of the Royal Opera and Gordon Eward of City Chambers."

"The message concludes: 'Meet me at 5 on...and then there is the image of a grid shaped like a leg. The symbol stands for St Luke on the Staffordshire Clog: 18 October, the Saturday Webb disappeared." I thought he was going to say "the day we found Webb's dead body," but Bell had his wits about him.

The note commanded the attention that Bell could hardly summon when talking straightforwardly. It was passed from hand to hand as though it were a holy relic. Paper was solid evidence, even though it was only a copy.

Just the same, M'Sween recognized it because he had seen the original. "So, Dr Bell," prompted Major Ross, "what is your reading of the complete note?"

"My rendering would be as follows:

> Troubles over 23 October (today, the day of the hanging). Take heart. Plans of 21 July (the date of the murders) well concluded. Meet me at 5 (that is 5 o'clock) on 18 October (the day of Webb's disappearance).
>
> Yours,
Andrew"

A hush followed this, broken at last by Andrew Burnham himself:

"What a gang of fools! Is there but one Andrew in all of Scotland? You look as though you have settled on my guilt. There's no health in it. I warn you. I am well able to defend myself. You shan't settle a noose around my neck on such flimsy testimony. I warn you all, I shall fight you! My father and I both will fight you. I bear the name of Burnham! It's a name that counts for something in this country. We've done signal service in this shire for many years. I shall not be put away without making a—"

"Hoots, lad, be still. Hear to what the man has to say. We'll protect you and the law will protect you. You have nowt to fear," said the old chief, who, I gathered, had known the young man from his childhood.

"The note was found in Webb's rooms. It connects Webb with guilty knowledge of the murders and to the murderer, Andrew Blank, shall we say, who then added Webb himself to his tally. From his point of view, it was a reasonable step to take: Webb had power over him because of what he knew. Far better to cut him off, thereby protecting himself from any chance of Webb changing his view of matters, whether by conscience or extortion. This note brought Webb to the rendezvous that resulted in his death. He invited himself to his victim's flat. He could never have got a dead body up all those stairs undetected. He also must have known before the murder about Webb's secret cupboard, where he kept various disguises, since he used it to hide the body in."

"Dr Bell," observed the Procurator-Fiscal, "you seem to be singularly well informed about these matters. Do you have an informer in fee at the station?"

"In time, you shall know all, sir. First, let me refer back to what I said earlier: we have all assumed that Mlle Clery was the intended victim of our murderer—even without the motive of robbery. I suggest to you that she was not. Eward, Gordon Eward, was the killer's target. Mlle Clery a very useful diversion, a smokescreen.

"Why Eward? Why the colourless bookkeeper? Because he was a particular colourless bookkeeper. He was murdered because he knew that Andrew Burnham had been pilfering from the public chest for some time. He had been speculating in the Tay Bridge scheme. As an honourable man, he went to Burnham and asked what he intended to do about it. Andrew asked for more time, promised to set matters to rights, and then he called upon Eward at the flat of his mistress. With Eward out of his road, he was able to cover his steps and, when caught in the act, pretended that it was Eward whose finances were in disarray. It was almost the perfect crime. No one suspected that his intended victim was more than a by-blow, an unlucky chance. His removal made it easy to cover his tracks."

"You have proofs for what you say, I hope, Doctor. You have made a serious allegation. Can you substantiate it?"

"Let me try." Here Bell turned to Mr Lambert, the father of Graeme, Alan and Louise. "Mr Lambert, on an evening not quite a week ago, you paid a visit to the Burnham house after receiving a note about my blundering into this investigation. Could you tell us about that?"

"It was some wiseacre's idea of a joke. It was a mistake. No one at the Burnham house was there to receive me. It was all ducks and drakes and to no purpose except to steal an hour of my peace."

"And who had signed the note you got?"

"Well, I thought it came from young Andrew, but he later denied sending it. It wouldn't have come from Sir William because we had had no conversation on the subject. Andrew has been most solicitous since Alan got in trouble. He assured me that everything possible was being done to save Alan and that amateurs—however well-meaning—might do more harm than good."

"Doyle, you will remember our visit to Webb's rooms? Here he turned to the old chief, and bowed. "I can see no harm in telling you this now, sir. We went to call upon Webb since he had been harassing us for some days. We knew that he was becoming worried about what we had uncovered so far." Here he turned back to me.

"Yes, sir. I remember it very well."

"Then you will recall that we discovered Webb's camera, a Thornton-Picard, and several exposed photographic plates?"

"Yes, some were pictures taken of me in front of the Parliament House. They must have been taken during the trial, before we had actively started looking into the case."

"Excellent! That coincides with my own memory exactly. At that time, before we had questioned the pawnbroker, which we did on the day the verdict was rendered, no one knew of our promise to help young Lambert, except Alan's brother, Graeme, from whom the request to help came. Tell us, Graeme, whom did you tell?"

Graeme looked a little stunned, as though he had been suddenly roused from sleep. He caught his father's face with the tail of his eye for a moment. "Why, I told my father and sister, Doctor."

"No one else?"

"No one else."

"Then, Mr Lambert, I turn to you. To whom did you impart this news?"

"I met Mr Burnham at my club. I knew his family of course. I was singularly touched by his greeting to me, under the circumstances. He asked if I had written to the Lord Advocate and I told him I had. I had just learned of Graeme's appeal to Dr Bell, and told him that too. I didn't see the harm, but he assured me that I would be blunting the edge of my appeal through normal channels. He suggested that bringing you into the matter would only put official backs up."

"Good! I'd guessed as much." Here he paused and looked from one face to the next until he had marshalled his remaining arguments. "You see, gentlemen, how often the name of Andrew Burnham comes into the story. It appears on a list of investors in his friend David M'Clung's Firth of Tay Bridge Company. The name Gordon Eward does not. I have suggested Andrew's motive. The company could not repay on schedule. His embezzlement had been discovered and would be exposed if he didn't do something about young Eward.

"To test my theory, I cabled Tom Prentice, Mlle Clery's former agent, in New York. I asked him to tell me the name of the man the police documents referred to as Mr XYZ. This is his reply, which I have not had time to read. Would you open the envelope and read the cable, Major Ross?"

The prison governor took the envelope from Bell and opened it while all of us watched. From it he removed a single piece of paper, which he unfolded and read in a low, rather hoarse voice:

DR JOSEPH BELL
FACULTY OF MEDICINE
UNIVERSITY OF EDINBURGH
THE NAME THAT HELENE ANDRE MENTIONED ON NIGHT OF MURDER, LATER CALLED MR XYZ BY POLICE, WAS ANDREW BURNHAM, SON OF SIR WILLIAM BURNHAM.

PRENTICE

THIRTY

The meeting in the gaol broke up shortly after the reading of the cable from Tom Prentice. Andrew Burnham was detained and, shortly afterwards, Keir M'Sween was swiftly relieved of his duties and likewise charged. He is now awaiting trial for complicity in concealing a crime and as an accessory after the fact. Andrew Burnham's trial for murder has been carried over until the spring assizes. Competent accountants, I have been told, have gone over his books for the past several years. They have been compared with the originals of the records left by Gordon Eward. Sir William has secured the services of Sir Henry Mildrew, QC, LLD, to lead his defence. The Lord Advocate has declined to prosecute the case personally. Sir William retired from public life as soon as the press began retailing the details of what I have been trying to record here.

The Lamberts went away, on a Pacific cruise. They returned overland, spending some time in Japan, China and India. Louise wrote to me at first every week. I delighted in experiencing the marvels of Bali and Samoa through her eyes. Then the letters stopped quite suddenly and were replaced by postal cards sent at rarer intervals as the family pursued its progress across the Mongolian desert and through the high mountain passes leading to India. From St Petersburg she wrote that she had met an American businessman and that their friendship was rapidly becoming something more. I steeled myself for her next letter, and when it came, I found I was still unprepared for its news. The marriage is to take place in San Francisco, where her

fiancé has a house overlooking the bay. I have no idea
which bay the house overlooks, but I intend to look it up
on a map of California one day.

Alan Lambert is now completely reconciled with his
father. In this I suspect the agency of his brother, Graeme,
and his sister. The poor man is cursed with two bohemian
sons. But now that Alan has sidestepped the gallows trap,
the unfortunate man protests that he is happy to have two
living sons be they as prodigal as can be. Perhaps it will
become easier for him to bear in the tropics so far from the
chilly wind that wraps itself around Edinburgh Castle. I
cannot help but sympathize with him.

Stevenson writes from America, from Monterey in
California:

> ...I have been tramping the hills above Carmel,
> but without the companionship of my dear Mod-
> estine...Here in the West, I am quite as brown as
> a crofter and happy as Larry. When I descend
> from the hills I am swept up into the generous
> bosom of the Osborne family, where I am trying
> to make a permanent place for myself beside my
> darling Fanny. At the moment, it's weddings (not
> mine) and cancelled weddings (again not mine)
> all too complicated to spout about...The Pacific
> is a rather peculiar sort of ocean and will require
> further study...

When I bought a printed copy of his book, I found that
Modestine was a donkey. His writing career is assured, or
so my literary friends say.

The terrible George Budd has written to me from Plymouth, urging me to join him there. He thinks I already
know enough medicine to support a shingle. I was tempted

to go, if only for the adventure of it, but Joe Bell has suggested that I postpone it until I have completed my studies
here. If it is adventure I crave, he suggests that I try to pass
myself off as a ship's doctor. He will write to the master of
a whaler that plies between here and Greenland. (I said
earlier that I was fated to be lost looking for Franklin's
bones.) It is a better, more practical idea, and, of course, I
must give it thought. Budd will wait, and, perhaps by the
time I am fully qualified, he will have discovered the cures
for all known diseases. If cocaine hasn't destroyed him first.

I wish I could say that Detective-Lieutenant Bryce was
received back into the bosom of the Edinburgh police force,
but some institutions, even when shaken to their roots, cannot change overnight. Bryce was on the brink of rejoining
the navy, when a cable arrived from Chicago in the United
States. It was an offer from Alan Pinkerton, who had established a private detecting agency, apart from his work with
the American government. Bryce was quick to accept this
offer from a fellow Scot and left this shore with few regrets.
From what I hear, he has made a great success of himself
doing the work he knows so well. He told me, in a recent
letter, that he now has an eighty-foot yacht which he keeps
at Alexandria on the Potomac River. For what it is worth,
he sounded content with his lot.

Marwood sent Bell a note offering to return his hospi-
tality should he ever find himself in Horncastle.

I am still torn between the practice of medicine and a
literary career. Bell says that he has been similarly tempted:
the new chief constable has been after him to consult upon
thorny problems of a curious nature, but so far he has only
commented upon them through the post. He tells me that
he is half-tempted to become—what does he call it?—a
consulting detective. He taunts the principal of the university with this thought from time to time, now that he has

become one of the living institutions of the faculty. I can well understand that lecturing to wave after wave of ignorant, opinionated young men can become tedious, but he takes some pleasure in turning young heads into wiser ones. Perhaps I too will resist the temptations that lie before me. I will neither rush off to Plymouth nor trade my scalpel for a pen just yet. Oh, I shall continue to write things and send them off to the journals, but I will not rush myself. Bell says that I have not yet found my subject. He is right there. But at least we both know that I am looking for it. The trick is to be able to recognize it when it comes along and to be ready.

The following items of recent information might serve to end this narrative. The first came in the afternoon post yesterday. It was an offer from *Chamber's Journal* to publish a story of mine, "The Mystery of Sasassa Valley," in a coming edition of that magazine. Naturally, I agreed. The second item of interest appeared in this afternoon's newspaper. Last night many people were killed when a railway bridge collapsed in a raging December storm, sending the engine, coaches, track and central span into the frigid waters below. It was the new Firth of Tay Bridge.

AFTERWORD

Thirty years after the story told in the foregoing pages, a man named Oscar Slater, a real eastern European immigrant to Glasgow, found himself in almost the same predicament as the fictional Alan Lambert. My story has used many aspects of the Slater case, as recorded in a number of versions by William Roughead. It is one of the most intriguing of British criminal proceedings and Roughead's telling of it has preserved for several generations of readers all of the inequities and ironies in this case of perverted justice. For this I owe him my thanks. Slater spent nearly twenty years in prison before the errors that put him there were officially, if grudgingly, acknowledged. Every step of the way, a stubborn legal establishment refused to admit its role in this wrongful or "wrongous," as they say in Scotland, conviction. In righting this wrong, no one was more vigorous than Sir Arthur Conan Doyle, by then— 1909–1929—an internationally famous writer. His sense of fair play and a belief in making the system work for all and not just for an isolated and privileged oligarchy turned Doyle into a real-life crime fighter. Conan Doyle was a fitting father of the consulting detective of 221B Baker Street. Although of a conservative disposition and very much a man of his time, Doyle's sense of justice often broke through convention in order to redress a wrong, such as in Slater's case.

Dr Joseph Bell is no fictional figment of my imagination. As a professor of surgery at Edinburgh University, he served as Doyle's mentor at the time of this novel. It was upon his amazing powers of observation and deduction that Doyle drew, in 1886, when he first wrote the name "Sherrinford Holmes" near the top of a page and then, later, adjusted the given name to "Sherlock." It was from the character of Doyle's friend George Budd that Doyle found clues to some of the more extravagant of Holmes's idiosyncrasies, which he discovered when he at last followed Budd and his bride to Plymouth.

Detective-Lieutenant Bryce is modelled on John Thomson Trench of the Glasgow police, who was detroyed by the established powers that ruled north of the Tweed. Having lost his career and his pension, as well as his reputation, he found useful work in the Royal Scots Fusiliers. But even here he was not safe; he was arrested on a trumped-up charge of receiving stolen goods, of which he was totally cleared after being held in custody for some months. Trench, clearly, was hounded to his grave by a vindictive, unforgiving oligarchy.

ACKNOWLEDGEMENTS

I would like to thank my friends at University College, University of Toronto, for their help in bringing this work into being. I would especially like to mention Lynd Forguson, Jack McLeod and A.P. Thornton. While in the vein, I should also thank my agent Beverley Slopen, my publisher Cynthia Good, my copy editor Mary Adachi, and my wife, Janet Hamilton, all of whom had something to do with the final shape of this novel.

The germ of this book began in a conversation with my friend the late Julian Symons. We were dining at Bofingers not far from La Place de la Bastille in Paris, when I mentioned the rough idea to him. He thought it interesting enough to pursue, although he doubted whether the Doyle family would thank me for trespassing upon the greatly esteemed name of Sir Arthur Conan Doyle. I assure them, and all, that this labour was undertaken in the same spirit with which Brigadier Girard swoops down on foxes and the celebrated consulting detective of 221B Baker Street entertains a fresh three-pipe problem.